The WITCH'S APPRENTICE

ALSO BY ZETTA ELLIOTT

Dragons in a Bag
The Dragon Thief

DRAGONS in a BAG
— BOOK 3 —

The WITCH'S APPRENTICE

ZETTA ELLIOTT

ILLUSTRATIONS BY CHERISE HARRIS

Random House  New York

Text copyright © 2022 by Zetta Elliott
Jacket art copyright © 2022 by Geneva B
Interior illustrations copyright © 2022 by Cherise Harris

Visit us on the Web! rhcbooks.com

Educators and librarians, for a variety of teaching tools, visit us at RHTeachersLibrarians.com

Library of Congress Cataloging-in-Publication Data
Names: Elliott, Zetta, author. | Harris, Cherise, illustrator.
Title: The witch's apprentice / Zetta Elliott; illustrations by Cherise Harris.
Description: First edition. | New York: Random House Children's Books, [2022]
Summary: Now that he is Ma's apprentice, Jax is finding himself mixed up with all sorts of magical doings, like taking care of a phoenix egg that is going to hatch soon, trying to bring back the creatures Sis stole, finding his grandfather, and convincing Sis, the guardian, to reunite the two realms—and hopefully living to see Brooklyn again.
Identifiers: LCCN 2021021448 | ISBN 978-0-593-42770-5 (trade) | ISBN 978-0-593-42771-2 (lib. bdg.) | ISBN 978-0-593-42772-9 (ebook)
Subjects: LCSH: African American boys—Juvenile fiction. | Magic—Juvenile fiction. | Witches—Juvenile fiction. | Apprentices—Juvenile fiction. | Phoenix (Mythical bird)—Juvenile fiction. | Brooklyn (New York, N.Y.)—Juvenile fiction. | CYAC: African Americans—Fiction. | Magic—Fiction. | Witches—Fiction. | Apprentices—Fiction. | Phoenix (Mythical bird)—Fiction. | Brooklyn (New York, N.Y.)—Fiction.
Classification: LCC PZ7.E45819 Wi 2022 | DDC 813.6 [Fic]—dc23

Printed in the United States of America
10 9 8 7 6 5 4 3 2 1
First Edition

The WITCH'S APPRENTICE

1

I keep having the same dream. Night after night I fall asleep knowing that I'll wake up sweating, with my heart racing and my hands curled into fists. Even after I'm wide awake, I hear a man whispering in my ear: "I've been waiting for you, my son."

Nobody calls me "son"—not anymore. Sometimes I wake up so upset that I can't tell what's sweat and what's tears. I wash my face in the bathroom and then try to fall back to sleep. Sometimes I can. Sometimes I can't.

I haven't told Mama. She's got enough to worry about, and talking about my father just makes her sad. Plus, she's a really sound sleeper, and I'm too old to be waking my mom up just because I had a bad dream. It's not really a nightmare, but I told Ma because I don't keep secrets from her. She's a good listener, and, well, she's a witch! So there's always a chance she'll be able to share her special knowledge with me.

Ma isn't my mother or my grandmother, like I once thought. We're not related at all, but right now Mama and I are living with Ma while our own apartment is being renovated. Now that school's out for the summer, I spend a lot more time with Ma. She has a thick *Book of Dreams* in her library, but Ma won't let me read it yet. Instead, she made me describe the dream over and over. Then she told me to write down all the details I could remember as soon as I woke up each night.

I don't see how that will help, but since I'm Ma's apprentice, I do as I'm told. Some nights the dream does change. Last week I felt the man's hand on my shoulder as he spoke—like he was standing behind me. But last night the hand was in front of me, reaching out from a fun house mirror that turned the man's body into a rubbery smear. I couldn't see his face, and I hate to admit it, but I don't remember what my dad's hands looked like. I remember how safe and strong I felt whenever he wrapped his fingers around mine, but that's it.

I'm busy writing all this in my Apprentice Journal when Ma knocks on the door with her cane.

"Ready?" she asks.

I nod and close my notebook, but Ma isn't there to

see it. I hear her shuffling down the long hallway that leads to the front door. Today Ma is wearing a bright orange bubble coat that's so puffy, it rubs against the wallpapered walls as she walks. She's got her purse slung over one shoulder and her folding stool tucked under her other arm. When Ma's got a job to do, she's totally focused and ready to get started with or without me. That's Rule #1: Always be ready.

I shove my notebook inside my knapsack before hustling down the hall after Ma. She's already outside the apartment waiting for the elevator, so I grab my sweatshirt and holler, "Bye, Mama!" over my shoulder as I slip out the front door.

"Got your gloves?" Ma asks. Her eyes are watching the illuminated numbers that show the elevator's ascent, but I take my gardening gloves out of my bag and wave them at her anyway. I have just enough time to pull my warmest hoodie over my long-sleeve T-shirt before the elevator bell rings, the doors open, and Ma nudges me inside. She passes her stool to me, and I hold it close to my chest. It's a tight squeeze with Ma's puffy orange coat taking up most of the space in the elevator, but soon we reach the ground floor and head over to the park.

My recurring dream isn't the only strange thing

that's happening around here. There's also something wrong with the weather. Summer in Brooklyn is usually sweltering, with lots of humidity and heat rising in waves off the concrete. But when Ma and I reach the park, nobody's wearing shorts or tank tops. It's too cold! Even the joggers are wearing tights, and one guy races by with earmuffs on! I don't blame him—it's the middle of July, but it feels more like the end of November.

Ambrose would be warm enough with his many layers of clothing, but he hasn't been stationed at the park entrance since last spring. Bro's gone, the guardhouses he protected no longer travel between realms, and Ma's turning me into a botanist instead of a witch. Almost every day we come to the park to forage. Fortunately, the cold weather has scared off all the bugs, but it's still no fun crawling all over the park while Ma stands over me pointing to different plants with her cane.

The first plant she taught me to spot was poison ivy. But turns out that's not the only plant that can make your skin itch. So I started wearing Mama's gardening gloves, and that helps, but foraging still isn't my favorite activity. Ma says being a witch is mostly about helping and healing. And making medicine from plants is one way to help folks heal. I get that—I really do. But when I decided to become Ma's apprentice, I thought I'd be doing something more . . . exciting.

I mean, Ma and I went back in time and saw dinosaurs! We found a special crystal, and I delivered baby dragons to the realm of magic. I know no job can be that exciting all the time, but . . . well, pulling up plants day after day is just boring! Ma won't even let me study the different plants listed in her books. All of a sudden, her entire library is off-limits.

I snuck into the living room last week and pulled one book off the shelf—*Shape & Substance: A Beginner's Guide to Transmogrification Spells*. I managed to smuggle the heavy tome into my bedroom without anyone noticing, but when I locked the door and opened the book, all the pages were blank! And I could hear Ma cackling with delight in the room next to mine. She outsmarts me every time.

Ma says I'm not ready to learn about the spells contained in those books. She insists that I need "hands-on training," but I'm the only one who's crawling around on their hands and knees. Ma supervises me while sitting comfortably on her collapsible stool that I carry to and from the park. I doubt her back aches as much as mine, but what bothers me most is, I don't feel like I'm learning anything important.

"What's that over there?" Ma asks after her long, loud yawn finally ends.

Since she's sitting a couple of feet behind me, I follow the general direction her cane's pointing and reach for a plant that has round, glossy leaves and tiny yellow flowers. "This one?" I ask.

"No!" she barks. "That other one."

I move my hand to the left and point at another plant. "This one?"

Ma sighs with impatience. "No! Look where I'm pointing, Jax."

I press my lips together so I won't say anything that might sound like sass. Mama taught me to respect my elders, and at her age, it's not like Ma can get down here in the dirt with me. So I just point my index finger and slowly move my arm from left to right. Ma grunts and sighs some more until I point at a strange purple plant with triangular leaves. It's nowhere near where she was pointing her cane, but Ma finally seems satisfied.

"*That's* the one," she says. "Pull it up gently, Jax, so you don't break off any of its roots. That's the part we need."

I do as I'm told and shake off the loose soil before handing the plant back to Ma. She sniffs the roots and even takes a small bite before placing it in a mesh bag.

"Good. Now keep your eyes peeled. We need a whole lot more of these."

"How many more?" I ask.

Ma shrugs and pulls her pipe out of her coat pocket. She taps a bit of ash out of the bowl and says, "A couple hundred should be enough."

Two hundred! I sit back on my heels and scan the grass around us for more purple triangular leaves. "I don't see any more, Ma."

She grunts and says, "That's 'cause you don't know how to look properly."

"Well, how am I ever gonna learn if you don't show me?" That's what I *want* to say, but I bite my tongue and say nothing instead. I don't know if witches can read minds, but Ma must know I'm feeling salty, because she suddenly suggests we take a break.

I happily yank off my gardening gloves and pull a granola bar out of my knapsack. Ma sticks the pipe in her mouth and searches her bag until she finds the mint tin that once held three baby dragons and then a feisty fairy. Ma flips open the lid and frowns when the tin turns out to be empty.

Ma grumbles as she leans forward on her stool to peer at the grass between us.

"What are you looking for?" I ask, even though I know the answer to that question might mean the end of my break.

"Gum grass," Ma says with a groan as she pushes back on her stool. "You found some for me last week, remember?"

I don't. But lately Ma has taken to smoking her

pipe every evening, so I must have found a lot of this particular plant. Mama thinks smoking a pipe sets a bad example, so Ma leans way out the kitchen window and blows the smoke into the alley behind our building. Gum grass doesn't smell like bubble gum—it's more like the spicy incense I smell at Vik's place sometimes. Once I went into the kitchen for a glass of water and heard Ma talking to someone in between puffs on her pipe. It was hard to see past her body, which filled up most of the window, but I'm pretty sure I saw a squirrel's fluffy tail waving above the fire escape railing.

"Ma!"

We both look across the meadow and see a park ranger making his way over to us on a mountain bike.

Ma waits till he's within earshot and then calls out, "Got anything for me, Cyrus?"

The ranger laughs and reaches into the pocket of his khaki coat. Rangers normally wear short-sleeve shirts and shorts in the summer, but not this year.

"Good morning to you, too," he says with a smile and a tip of his funny dented hat. "I was going to offer you the pleasure of my company, but I found this last week and suspect you might prefer it."

The ranger winks at me before handing a small white

envelope to Ma. She peeks inside and then beams up at Cyrus. "Gum grass!"

"Found a patch of it growing over by the Nethermead meadow—some good mushrooms, too, if you're interested."

"No time for mushrooms today," Ma says while packing a bit of gum grass into her pipe. "We're on a mission."

"Top secret?" the redheaded ranger asks.

"Naturally," Ma says with a wink.

Cyrus turns to me. "Then this must be your accomplice."

"Actually, I'm Ma's apprentice," I tell him.

Cyrus's eyebrows go up, and I realize too late that he probably doesn't know that Ma's a witch. Ma glares at me before forcing a fake laugh to distract the ranger.

"Jax has been helping me gather some wild silver root. How you been feeling, Cy? You look tired."

"Tell you the truth, Ma, I've been under the weather the past couple of days. No fever or body ache," he explains. "I just feel worn-out."

"I thought a little fresh air would perk me up, but I'm feeling kind of drowsy myself. Why don't you take a couple days off, Cy—get some rest," Ma suggests.

The ranger shakes his head and stifles a yawn. "Can't— we've already got five people who called in sick this week. Seems to be spreading all over the city. Strange, huh? Just one symptom: fatigue."

Ma sucks on her pipe and studies Cyrus for a moment. Then she reaches into the mesh bag we've been filling and pulls out the purple plant with the triangular leaves. Ma snaps off a length of root and blows on it. She pops half into her own mouth before offering the rest to the ranger.

"Here—chew on this."

Cyrus turns it over before popping it into his mouth. The root must be bitter, because he crinkles his nose and then takes a drink of water from the bottle clipped to his bike. "Whew! That's got quite a kick."

"Silver root is a natural stimulant. A little of that root goes a long way. Keep an eye out for it when you're making your rounds. Get some to your coworkers if you can."

"Will do," the ranger says, looking more alert already. "Thanks, Ma," he adds with genuine gratitude.

"Right—break time's over, Jax." Ma leans heavily on her cane and eases herself off the collapsible stool. "Time to head home."

A moment ago, Ma said we needed to pull up a couple hundred silver root plants, but if she's changed her mind, I'm not about to argue. I fold her stool and tuck it under my arm. Cyrus waves as he pedals off.

"I gotta make a call," Ma says with a frown.

Unlike most people, Ma doesn't have a cell phone that she can carry in her purse. Instead, she's got an old-fashioned rotary phone that doesn't actually plug into the wall. I've only seen her use it once before.

"Do you need to talk to L. Roy?" I ask. I met L. Roy in the realm of magic last spring. He's the one who mailed Ma three baby dragons from Madagascar.

Ma shakes her head and doesn't seem to notice when something small and white falls off her Afro.

My first thought is *Does Ma have dandruff?* But it would be rude to say that, so instead I ask, "Is that snow?"

Ma sticks out her hand, and within a few seconds, several tiny flakes drift down from the sky and land on her palm. They don't melt when she rubs them between her fingers.

"Not snow," I conclude.

Ma sniffs at the white bits and then blows them away. "Hmm."

"Feathers?" I guess next.

Ma shakes her head and starts heading toward the park exit. "It's ash."

Ma complains about her knees a lot, but with the help of her cane, she can move pretty fast when she wants to. I hustle to keep up. When we reach the street, Ma doesn't turn right. Instead, she heads north—away from our building.

"I thought you needed to make a phone call," I remind her.

"I want to check something before we head home."

I follow Ma along Empire Boulevard and think about my grandfather as we pass the fast-food place where he got us burgers last spring. That was the first time we ever met, but we hit it off right away. Trub and Mama don't always see eye to eye, but they're learning to trust each other again. When my granddad's around, I feel like my family's whole again. Nothing can take the place left by my dad, but now with Ma and Trub and a little magic, my life feels a lot fuller.

I haven't seen Trub much lately. Ma says he's become Sis's right-hand man, and that my granddad will be around more once Ma retires and goes to live with Sis in the realm of magic. Whenever I ask her when she plans to retire, Ma just looks off in the distance and says, "Soon." I guess that's when I'm going to see my grandfather again.

My stomach growls as we pass another burger joint and the doughnut shop as well. Ma turns up Franklin Avenue, and that's when I realize she's heading for the spice factory. That's what it is in the real world, at least. The brick building is covered in graffiti, and half the windows are boarded up. But last spring, when my friend Kenny decoded the magic writing on the outside of the building, it turned into Esmeralda's Excellent Emporium of Exotic Spices, Magical Potions, and Mythical Creatures of All Kinds. Blue was brewing smelly stuff inside, and that's also where he held Vik's sister and aunt hostage.

The brick smokestack is still standing, and for the first time, it seems to be in use. I stand next to Ma and remember how Sis left the realm of magic to reclaim the baby dragon that Kavita tried to keep for herself. Blue was hiding creatures on his body as tattoos, and Sis claimed them, too. Before returning to her own realm, Sis gave me a potion that cured Ma of her sleeping sickness. We had to say goodbye to some of our friends, but I still feel proud when I think about that night. Now I stare up at the smokestack and wonder why Ma's frowning again.

"You okay, Ma?" I ask finally.

She grunts and brushes a few white flakes off my shoulder before asking, "How 'bout you, Jax? You feel okay?"

"Yes, ma'am."

Ma grunts again before turning away from the spice factory and heading in the direction of home. I'm about to follow her, when I see a flutter of black wings on top of the chain-link fence.

"Soot?" I call, but it's not my pigeon friend. It's a giant crow that caws loudly at me before flying off. I hurry after Ma and hear her muttering something under her breath.

"Shoulda known he was up to no good."

"Who?" I ask. Then I shiver and glance at the park across the street. Two elderly men are playing chess, but I don't see anyone else. I still cautiously whisper, "Do you mean Blue?"

The last time I saw him, Blue did say he wasn't ready to give up on his mission to keep magical creatures in the real world. Sis stripped him of his entire collection, but Blue said there were other people who shared his point of view. Were they still running the emporium?

"That weasel's been operating right under our noses," Ma says, her lips twisted in disgust. "Soon as we get home, I'm gonna need you to pack your bag, Jax."

I nod and allow myself just one more question. "Er . . . where are we going?"

Ma stops walking and glares at me but in a way that lets me know she's not really mad. "You really have to ask? For weeks you've been begging me to take you to the annual convention."

"Chicago!" I clamp a hand over my mouth to keep the rest of my excitement inside.

Ma starts walking and talking really fast. I'm so happy, I practically skip the rest of the way home.

"We'll need a day or two to get everyone organized, but I can't leave you here on your own. It's too risky. Whatever that fool's concocted doesn't seem to bother youngsters, but you never know. . . ."

Ma looks up at the sky and sighs heavily as the white fluff drifts down around us. "You tell your little friends to stay inside as much as possible. Don't tell 'em why— just say it's important. There's no need to panic . . . yet." Ma stops and bars my way forward with her cane. "Can you do that, Jax?"

I stop jumping around and wipe the "I'm going to Chicago!" grin off my face. "Yes, ma'am."

Ma nods and pushes me forward with her cane. "Then let's get going. It's time for us to leave New York."

2

Mama's eyebrows are mashed together like two warring caterpillars. I can't tell if she's actually angry or simply confused by everything we've just told her. Mama doesn't like magic, but she's learned to accept that the rest of her family feels differently. Ma is cleaning her teeth with a toothpick. It's clear she doesn't want to rush Mama into making a decision, and neither do I. I don't have a toothpick, so I just keep my fingers crossed under the kitchen table and hope Mama agrees to let me leave with Ma for Chicago tomorrow morning.

Pushing back her chair, Mama sighs as she stands to gather the plates. I jump up to help clear the table, and as I reach the sink, I hear her say, "If it's as bad as you say it is, Ma, then Jaxon will be better off with you. I guess I'll be on my own for a few days."

I set the glasses in the sink and pump my fist just once. When I turn around, Mama's shaking her head at me, but there's a little smile on her lips that lets me know she knows how much this trip means to me.

"You be on your best behavior, Jaxon. Do everything Ma tells you to do, and call me if you need anything."

"Call you?"

Now's not the time to ask Mama for a phone of my own, but she surprises me by pulling my dad's phone out of her pocket. I know she still listens to the greeting on his voicemail sometimes.

"Take this. Remember to keep it fully charged," she says.

The screen is cracked, but Dad's smartphone still works. I reach for it, and for a moment Mama and I stand there at the kitchen counter, the thin black phone like a bridge keeping us connected. Then Mama lets go, and I'm the only one holding on to this precious piece of my father.

Mama steps around me and turns the hot water on full blast. Clouds of steam rise from the sink, but they can't hide the emotion in my mother's face. I wrap my arms around her waist and hold on for a little while.

Finally, Ma says, "Time to pack, boy. And don't forget

what I told you about getting that message to your friends."

I nod and take my father's phone back to my room. Vik is the first person I call, but when I hear his voice, he sounds upset.

"Can I come over—like, right now?" Vik asks urgently.

"Sure—are you okay?"

"I'll tell you everything when I get to your place. Meet me downstairs."

"Will do," I reply, but Vik doesn't hear me because he has already hung up. It'll take him a while to walk over to Ma's building, so I call Kenny next. He's laughing so hard, he can hardly speak. Vik and I used to think Kenny was a bully, but we got to know him better last spring. Kenny *is* big and strong, but he's smart, too. He's the one who figured out a way to open Ma's tin with the fairy inside. Kenny's been kind of glum since Jef went back to the realm of magic, so it's surprising to hear him laughing so hard.

"Kenny? Kenny, calm down. I have to tell you something. It's serious. Kenny!"

Finally, Kenny stifles his laughter enough to listen to me. "Ma says you need to stay inside for the next few days. Can you do that?"

Kenny cracks up again but manages to say, "Sure, Jax. No problem. I'm mostly hanging out in my shed anyway."

"Don't you want to know why you need to stay indoors?" I ask.

Kenny clears his throat and says, "It's got something to do with magic, right?"

"Right. But not the good kind. Blue's up to something. I was at the factory today and—"

"Whoa!"

I can't tell whether Kenny dropped the phone or just found something else to laugh at, but after a few attempts at calling his name, I end the call. I poke my head into the kitchen to say I'm meeting Vik downstairs.

Mama's sitting across the table from Ma once more. Both of Mama's hands are folded over Ma's. I can tell by the look on her face that that kind of contact makes Ma uncomfortable, but she just bows her head and listens as Mama talks in a low voice.

I won't be long, so I decide not to disturb them and quietly let myself out of the apartment. When I get downstairs, I see Vik pacing back and forth in front of the building.

As soon as he sees me, Vik thrusts a package at me and says, "Here—take this! I can't keep it anymore. It's not safe—not when my sister's such a . . . a . . . I don't even know *what* she is! I mean, she's always been a bit of a brat, but now she's seriously dangerous!" Vik throws his hands up and yells at the sky, "Argh! I can't believe this is happening!"

I've never seen my friend so upset, but I do my best to calm him down. "Take it easy, Vik. Slow down and start from the beginning. What's Kavita done now?"

Vik sits down on the low brick wall that surrounds the flower garden in front of Ma's building. He sighs heavily and says, "She's always been weird—you know that. And I know she misses Aunty—we all do. So at first I thought she was just . . . I don't know. Mourning? Moping? But then I went into her room one morning, and she wasn't sleeping in her bed."

"Where was she?"

"On the floor, Jax! Curled up like a cat. So I went over and touched her leg—lightly—with my toe. I didn't kick her or anything. But she made this sound . . . it was like a low growl. At first, I thought it was her stomach, and so I laughed. And that's when she woke up."

"And?"

Vik shudders and presses his own eyes shut. "It wasn't Kavi, Jax. The *thing* sleeping on the floor that growled at me . . . it wasn't my little sister anymore."

21

I shiver and pull my hood over my head.

Vik takes a deep breath to steady his nerves before continuing. "She only opened one eye. But, Jax—it wasn't a human eye. It was . . . like the eye of a lizard."

"A lizard!" I exclaim.

"Or . . . a dragon."

If Vik didn't look so serious, I'd think he was pulling my leg. All I can think to say is "No way . . ."

Thinking I don't believe him, Vik hurries on. "I know—it sounds weird, but I swear I'm not making this up. I started to back away from her—it—and that's when I tripped over Aunty's birdcage. I guess that startled her or something, because Kavi came back. She sat up and rubbed her eyes, and when she opened them . . . they were back to normal! But I know what I saw, Jax. I don't know why or how, but I think my little sister is turning into someone—or something—else."

I sink onto the wall next to Vik and try to gather my thoughts. The first thing I ask is "Have you seen Kenny lately?"

"No. Why?"

"I think something strange is going on with him, too. Can you stop by and see if he's all right?"

"I'll try, but I can't stay out too long. I have to keep an eye on my sister. There's something else you need to know. It's the real reason I'm here—why I needed to give you that package *now*."

"What is it, Vik?"

He ignores my question and says, "Kavi opened her mouth to yell at me yesterday, and . . . uh . . . *smoke* came out of her mouth. And you know as well as I do that where there's smoke . . ."

"There's fire! You think your sister can actually breathe fire?"

"I don't want to find out! She's real moody these days, and if she doesn't get her way, she acts like a big baby."

"A big baby dragon, you mean."

"The only thing that seems to calm her down is peda, but Aunty's not around to make it, and Mummy hasn't gone to the sweetshop for more. I'm giving Kavi every kind of candy I can find—I even dug into my Halloween stash."

I blink at him. "Seriously? You still have candy left over from last Halloween?"

Vik snaps his fingers in my face. "Focus, Jax! What's going to happen when I run out?"

"You *can't* run out. I don't have any Halloween candy left, but I'm pretty sure Ma's got a bag of marshmallows upstairs. I'll go get it for you."

"Jax—wait!"

Vik grabs my arm and pulls me back down onto the wall.

"I need to tell you something else. Something I did a while ago . . . when I was just a kid. I mean, I'm still a kid, and I'm not trying to make excuses. I know what I did was wrong. . . ."

I sigh. I don't know how many more revelations I can take. It feels like everything in my world has been turned upside down today!

"Just tell me, Vik—whatever it is. You helped me when I told you I left Ma in the Jurassic period and again when I lost a baby dragon."

I meant to make Vik feel better, but instead, he scowls and says, "You didn't lose it—Kavi stole it!"

"What I'm trying to say is, you don't have to feel bad if you've made some kind of mistake, too."

Vik nods and takes a deep breath. "You're my best friend, Jax. But before we met, I used to hang out with Carlos and Tariq."

"I remember. You three had a pretty wild summer last year, right?"

"R-right. I told you about the phoenix we found behind that boarded-up brownstone."

"Yeah—and how it started a big fire when the Pythons started messing with you guys."

Vik nods and looks down at his feet, clearly embarrassed. "Well, that's not the whole story. I left something out. Something major."

"And the major thing you left out . . . is in this bag?" I ask.

Vik nods, but when I try to open the bag, he stops me. "Wait till you're alone—and somewhere safe. Somewhere cool. Somewhere far away from fire."

I must look confused, because Vik finally stands up and looks me in the eye. "When a phoenix reaches the end of its life, it sets a big fire and expires in the flames."

"I know. And then the new phoenix rises from the ashes."

"That's what all the stories say," Vik confirms. "But after the fire last summer, we never found the new phoenix. We turned the empty lot into a community garden. And it was great—everybody in the neighborhood helped out, and we shared all the fruits and vegetables and flowers we grew together."

"Sounds cool," I tell him.

"It was. Until . . . one day I was pulling up weeds, and when I reached around this giant eggplant . . . I found something strange. I didn't know what it was—I'm still not entirely sure—but I think it's . . . an egg."

My eyes open wide. "THE egg?"

Vik nods. "I think so. It looks like a burnt tennis ball, except . . . it hums."

I hold the paper bag up to my ear. Vik's right. There's a soft buzzing sound coming from the bag. "Why do you think the baby phoenix hasn't hatched yet?"

"I don't know. I should have shown it to Carlos and Tariq, but I took it home instead so I could study it. It wasn't humming then, and I kind of just forgot about it."

"Where have you been keeping it?" I ask.

"In my sock drawer." My eyebrows go up, and Vik shrugs. "What? It had to be somewhere Kavi would never look. She's so nosy—she goes through my stuff all the time."

I don't think I could forget that I had a baby phoenix hidden in my sock drawer. "So you figured it was safe . . . until your sister started to turn into a fire-breathing dragon."

"Right. I thought maybe you could show it to Ma or your granddad, and they'd know what to do."

I nod. "We leave for Chicago tomorrow. That reminds me—Ma told me to tell you to stay inside as much as you can."

"Why?"

"Looks like Blue's burning something over at the old

26

spice factory. Whatever's coming out of the smokestack is having a strange effect on people—adults mostly. Ma wants you to avoid the falling ash in case it starts to affect kids, too."

Vik's eyes open wide. "Whoa. I'll go see Kenny and then head straight home."

"Thanks, Vik. I'll have my dad's phone with me in Chicago, so you can call or text me in case . . ." I pause and try to think of something that won't alarm my friend. "In case anything changes."

Vik nods and shoves his empty hands in his pockets. I hold the bag with the phoenix egg in my hands, and we stand there awkwardly for a few seconds. I wish I could stay and support Vik the way he stayed by my side when I had problems with the baby dragons. I kind of want to give him a hug and tell him everything's going to be okay, but I don't know that everything *will* be okay. So instead, I just raise my hand and say, "See ya, Vik."

He gives me another grim nod and heads for Kenny's place. I stuff the paper bag into the front pocket of my hoodie and go back upstairs. Mama and Ma are still huddled together in the kitchen, so I decide to wait and tell Ma about the egg tomorrow. It's not urgent, and she's got Blue to worry about.

I go into my room and check my overnight bag for

the sixth time. I don't need much for a three-day trip, so there's plenty of room for Vik's egg. When I'm sure no one's in the hallway, I pull the paper bag from my pocket and allow myself a quick look. I stuff the egg into my overnight bag, next to my socks but then decide it's best to keep it on me. If the airline loses my bag or someone tries to snatch it, then I'll lose the egg and let Vik down. And I can't let that happen. Vik's counting on me.

I put on my pajamas and push the paper bag under my pillow. The strange buzzing is muffled, and before long it lulls me to sleep. In my dreams I hear the strange man telling me the same thing: "I've been waiting for you, my son."

3

I wake up at least an hour before everyone else and lie in bed wondering how I'll get the phoenix egg past airport security. But when Ma finally gets up, I ask her about calling a taxi, and she tells me we aren't heading to JFK or LaGuardia.

"We're not flying to Chicago?"

"Nope. Go eat your breakfast, boy."

I want to tell Ma about Vik's egg, but instead, I just put it back in my hoodie's front pocket and do as I'm told. Since I'm leaving today, I let Mama fuss over me in the kitchen. She's made my favorite banana pancakes with scrambled eggs and crispy fake bacon. When I can't eat another bite, Mama takes away my plate and tells me to brush my teeth. I keep the bathroom door open so I can hear the doorbell ring.

Ma says we're going to Chicago with three of her

friends. There are about a dozen witches in the New York City coven, but apparently the ones from Brooklyn always travel together. Will they all be as old as Ma? I'm kind of hoping at least one of the other witches will have a young apprentice like me.

Ma taps on the bathroom door with her cane and tells me to hurry up. I grab my knapsack from my bedroom and find only Ma and Mama waiting for me at the front door.

"Where are your friends?" I ask.

"They'll meet us at the usual rendezvous spot," Ma replies.

"So . . . if we're not flying, I guess that means we're taking the train. What time do we need to be at Penn Station?" I ask.

"We're not leaving from Penn Station."

I try again. "Grand Central?"

"Nope."

Ma just nods at Mama instead of saying goodbye and goes out to the hall to wait for the elevator. Mama smothers me with too many kisses and a too-long, too-tight hug. I promise—for the hundredth time—to listen to Ma and call home every night before bed. Then it's my turn to remind Mama to stay inside as much as possible and chew on the chopped-up silver

31

root Ma gave her if she starts to feel drowsy. I hold up Dad's phone and take a selfie with my mom. I text it to her right away so she can look at it whenever she misses me.

Ma grows impatient and hollers, "Hurry up, boy!"

I hustle out the door before Mama can hug me again and slip inside the elevator. Ma pulls back her cane, and the doors slide shut on Mama's tearstained face.

"You been away from home before?" Ma asks.

"Once—for summer camp. But . . . that was before my dad died."

"You and your mama are real close. I can tell," Ma says softly.

I nod and look down at the selfie I just took on my dad's phone. I'll only be gone for a few days. I tell myself that Mama will be fine—and I'll be fine, too.

I put the phone in my back pocket and focus on the matter at hand. "Are we taking a bus from Port Authority?"

Ma sighs, but she looks more amused than annoyed. "Boy, will you quit fussing 'bout how we're getting to Chicago? We're not taking a plane, train, or automobile. But the UR should get us there in no time."

"The . . . er?"

"I'm not answering one more question," Ma says as

we exit the elevator. "Just keep your mouth shut and your eyes open. All will be revealed in time."

Part of being a good apprentice is following orders, so I do as I'm told and follow Ma up the block. Everything I need for the trip fit inside my knapsack, so I offer to pull Ma's small suitcase, since my hands are free. When we pass the subway station and enter Prospect Park, I don't say a word. It looks like we're heading for the Boathouse, but we can't sail to Chicago . . . can we?

I swallow all my questions, and when Ma stops next to an old-fashioned lamppost, I stand beside her and gaze up at the flickering flame. I didn't know they had gas lamps in the park, but this secluded spot does make an ideal rendezvous point. Either we're early or the other witches are late, because Ma and I are the only ones around. I wait to see what will happen, keeping Rule #1 at the front of my mind.

Ma opens her purse and pulls out her pocket watch. She checks the time and frowns.

"I expect that young gal to be late, but not Mrs. B. And your grandfather's usually on time."

I gasp. "Trub's coming with us?"

"That's the plan," Ma replies, chuckling as I practically leap with joy. "We'll give them a few more minutes and then head downstairs to the platform."

I nod at Ma and wonder if now's a good time to tell her about the egg in my pocket. But Ma seems kind of distracted, and now that Trub will be joining us, I can wait and tell my grandfather instead. To pass the time, I silently try to piece together the clues Ma has given me so far. Trains leave from a platform, but we already passed the subway, and Ma said we're not leaving from New York's two main train stations. We're standing on a path that's paved with hexagonal stones. Lullwater Bridge isn't far from here, which means we're close to the lake, but boats leave from a dock, not a platform. I'm also not sure how we could go downstairs from here without going underground, but since I can't ask any more questions, I'll have to wait until Ma offers an explanation.

After a couple more minutes pass, Ma sighs irritably and slips her pocket watch into her purse. "Come on, boy. I don't know what's keeping them, but we can't leave Dutch waiting down there in the dark."

The lamppost is next to a short tunnel. When we get halfway through it, Ma suddenly stops walking. She holds her cane up to the wooden planks that line the curved walls and taps several times.

"My memory ain't what it used to be," Ma says with a frown. "Which one is it?"

I would offer to help, but to do that, I'd have to ask at least one question. So instead, I wait for Ma to ask me for assistance. She keeps tapping the planks up high and down low with her cane until one in the middle of the wall makes a hollow sort of sound. Ma grins and pushes the tip of her cane straight into that particular beam. It slides inward several inches, and then the stone tiles near our feet start to move, too!

I jump back and check both ends of the tunnel to see if anyone is headed our way. Thankfully, the coast is clear, and there's no one else to witness the formation of a spiral staircase as the hexagonal paving stones sink into the earth to form steps.

When the stones stop moving, Ma prods me with her cane. "Go on. What you waiting for?"

I peer into the shadowy staircase and try to sound braver than I feel. "It's kind of dark down there." Then I remember that I've got my dad's phone and pull it out of my pocket. "Good thing I have a light on my phone."

Ma nods, and I think I see a touch of pride tugging at the corner of her mouth. I lower the extended handle of her suitcase and pick it up. With the phone in my other hand, I slowly ease down the staircase, noticing how the temperature drops as we descend. I manage to light the steps in front of me, but when the staircase ends,

we're in a cavern so vast that my phone can't push back the darkness.

Ma turns her cane over and blows on its tip, and instantly it becomes a torch. She holds it above her head and searches the shadows. "You there, Dutch?"

Suddenly, we hear a shriek from above, and a pink suitcase tumbles down the spiral staircase, narrowly missing Ma when it crashes to a halt at the bottom.

"Reckless girl!" a woman exclaims irritably.

"I'm sorry. It was an accident!"

"It's those ridiculous shoes you have on your feet. You should have worn something sensible."

"'Sensible' might be your style, Mrs. B., but it's definitely not mine. These are my traveling boots. I never leave home without them."

Ma swings the light over to the staircase so we can see who's bickering. The first thing I see is a pair of pointy-toed, high-heeled silver-and-white-snakeskin boots. The young woman wearing the boots struggles to navigate the small stone steps, but she finally manages to reach the ground. She sighs with satisfaction and smooths her colorful dress before reaching back to take the worn carpetbag from the hands of the older woman behind her.

"Thank you, Quayesha," the woman says. She has a Caribbean accent like Mama's friend Afua.

"No problem, Mrs. B. Now, where's *my* suitcase?"

I set it upright and pull up the extendable handle before wheeling it over to the young woman. She gives me a warm smile and says, "Why, thank you, kind sir. You must be Jaxon. I'm Quayesha."

She holds out her hand, and as we shake, at least a dozen silver hoops jangle around her wrist. Quayesha looks like the women I saw in downtown Brooklyn when Mama took me to DanceAfrica. The performances were mostly inside the Brooklyn Academy of Music, but the street outside was just as lively, with drummers and vendors selling food, art, jewelry, and clothes from all over the continent.

"You look like Africa," I tell her, and then blush as I stumble over my words. "I mean DanceAfrica—your dress reminds me of ones I saw at that festival. It's really nice."

Quayesha lets go of my hand and holds up her skirt to curtsy. "Aren't you charming! I can see why Ma brags about you so much. Maybe I should get an apprentice, too."

"Ha! You'd just make him hold your bags while you shopped for clothes," Ma says.

"Actually, I made this dress myself. It only looks like

haute couture." Quayesha winks at me, and I smile back at her.

Not Ma. She just shakes her head as her eyes sweep over Quayesha's not-so-practical travel outfit. The other woman stands next to Ma, her lips pushed out in a way that lets us know she also disapproves of the stylish young witch.

Aware that she's being judged, Quayesha twirls to show off her dress from all angles. By the light of Ma's torch, the gold waves on the waxy purple fabric shimmer as she spins. Her long dreadlocks whirl around her like the carousel swing ride at Luna Park. There are cowrie shells, small crystals, and copper rings woven into her long black hair. Spinning in the shadows, Quayesha looks magical—at least to me.

She ends her fashion show by planting her hands on her hips like a model at the end of the runway. The tiny diamonds embedded in the tips of her long acrylic fingernails sparkle like stars. "Just say the word, Mrs. B., and I'll make you a dress, too. We could do a total makeover—hair, clothes, accessories. . . ."

The older woman loudly sucks her teeth and pulls together her drab woolen cardigan. It matches her long, shapeless skirt, which looks like it could be gray or brown.

Ma looks just as frumpy in her puffy orange coat, purple velour tracksuit, and black sneakers. She rolls her eyes at Quayesha and says, "Mrs. Benjamin isn't interested in 'haute couture,' and neither am I."

Quayesha looks at the older women with pity. "But your clothes are so . . . ordinary."

"That's because we are trying to blend in," Mrs. Benjamin says in a stern voice. "You, on the other hand, seem determined to attract attention to yourself. A witch should walk through the world with humility and discretion."

Quayesha pouts and says, "I can be humble, discreet, *and* cute at the same time!"

Mrs. Benjamin groans. "Give me strength. . . ."

Ma pulls out her pocket watch again. "Anybody hear from Dutch? It's not like her to be this late."

It's not like Trub, either. Mrs. Benjamin starts explaining to Ma her theory about Dutch's warped perception of time.

"The poor thing actually believes she can stop the hands of time. When I asked her how exactly, she started throwing out all sorts of impossible words—'quantum' this, and 'polychronic' that. . . ."

Ma doesn't really seem interested, but she listens patiently as Mrs. Benjamin compares African and Western time. Quayesha turns to me and makes a funny face. I smother a giggle and make sure Ma doesn't see me snickering.

Quayesha leads me a few steps away from the others and says, "You're awful quiet, Jax. Aren't you excited about our trip to Chicago?"

I nod enthusiastically and glance over at Ma. She's busy debating Mrs. Benjamin, so I dare to tell Quayesha the truth. "Ma told me to stop asking questions."

She laughs, and her silver bangles ring like bells. "Well, that may be Ma's rule, but you can ask me anything. How else are you supposed to learn the ropes?"

I'm liking Quayesha more and more. "What's the 'er'?"

"It's an abbreviation—a quicker way to say Underground Railroad. U.R. *UR*."

I can't believe it. "*That's* how we're getting to Chicago?" I exclaim.

I guess the skepticism in my voice draws Ma's attention, because she calls out, "You got a problem with that, boy?"

I blink and press my lips together so I don't speak before I think. But after a few seconds of silence, I just can't keep my words inside, and they fly out of my mouth.

"The Underground Railroad isn't real!"

Mrs. Benjamin gasps, and I realize I might be making

Ma—my boss—look bad. So I try to explain myself and show how much I know. "I mean, it *is* real—or it *was*. But it wasn't an *actual* railroad, and people didn't really travel underground. They just called it that because it was supposed to be secret—an invisible way for folks to move from slave states in the South to free states in the North. But slavery ended a long time ago."

I thought that was a pretty good explanation, but everyone is staring at me like I'm not making any sense. I try to stay calm, but finally I blurt out: "We can't get to Chicago that way!"

"Well, that's how we're going," Ma says firmly. "You can stay here in Brooklyn with your mama if that's what you prefer."

Ma points over at the staircase, but I shake my head and say, "No, ma'am. I want to go with you."

Ma snaps her fingers, and the staircase unravels as the paving stones float back up to once again form the interlocking floor of the tunnel. I open my mouth to apologize, since it's clear I've done something wrong, but Ma holds up her finger to silence me.

"We three have been doing this a long time, Jax. You've only been at it for a couple of months. What's Rule #1?"

"Always be ready."

Ma nods. "Well, here's Rule #2: Trust your elders. How old are you, boy?"

Ma knows how old I am, so I guess this is for the benefit of everybody else. "I'll be ten in October," I say quietly.

Mrs. Benjamin sucks her teeth. "October is months away! The correct answer is, you are nine years old."

Ma nods. "Listen, Jax. Every witch here is older than you. Every witch here has more experience than you. Your role—in Brooklyn and on this trip—is to *assist*, not to instruct. Think you can handle that?"

My cheeks feel like they're burning brighter than the torch Ma's holding above her head. I manage to squeak out, "Yes, ma'am," before my throat closes completely.

Then I think about how Mama comes home angry sometimes because her coworker Jay insisted on explaining something she already understood. "It's such a waste of time," Mama told me, "but some men believe they know more than a woman ever could." It happens so often, there's even a name for it: *mansplaining*. Was I kidsplaining just now? If I was, that's not cool, so I add, "Sorry, Ma. Sorry, everybody."

Mrs. Benjamin sniffs and says, "Personally, I have always felt that children should be seen and not heard."

Quayesha puts her arm around my shoulders and

gives me a quick squeeze. She leans down and whispers, "Don't sweat it, kid. I made a lot of mistakes, too, when I started my training."

That makes me feel a bit better, but I still decide to put a little space between me and Ma. I wheel her suitcase close to the edge of the circle of torchlight and sit down on it. I wonder what's keeping Trub. I'd feel a lot better if my grandfather was here. Trub's always got my back.

I pull out my dad's phone and check the time. Hopefully, Trub will get here sooner rather than later.

4

"Psssst! Kid—hey, kid!"

I know that voice! I look around but can't see anything moving in the shadows. "Nate?"

"Behind you, kid."

I spin so fast, I almost topple off Ma's suitcase. Nate the rat pokes his head out from behind a small boulder that's embedded in the wall of the cavern. I beam at him and ask, "What's up, Nate? Are you coming with us to Chicago?"

"Can't, kid. Too much going on around here. Gotta keep my ear to the ground."

Nate checks to ensure that the others are distracted before coming closer. "Listen, Trub asked me to pass along a message. He really wanted to take you to Chicago, but something came up."

My heart sinks. "He's not coming?"

Nate shakes his head. "He would if he could, kid, but Sis needs him."

"I need him, too." That's what I *want* to say, but there's nothing Nate can do. Sis gets what Sis wants. I sigh and thank Nate for letting me know.

"Sorry to be the bearer of bad news," he says. "Can I offer you a piece of advice before you go?"

"Sure—I need all the advice I can get. Seems like I keep saying and doing the wrong thing."

Nate checks again to make sure that the others can't hear us. He waves me closer, so I lean in. "Word on the street is, you ain't the only one getting outta town."

"What do you mean?"

"Nobody's seen Blue. I thought maybe he was laying low after Sis humiliated him last spring. But I think he's skipped town—for good this time."

"Are you sure? Ma thinks Blue's up to something at the old spice factory."

"Oh, he's definitely up to no good—you can bet on that. But he's not working alone anymore. He's got some powerful allies, so watch yourself, kid."

"I will," I assure him. "Thanks for the heads-up, Nate."

"Sure, kid. Now, about that egg you got in your pocket . . ."

I gasp and glance over at the witches. It sounds like

they've decided to call Dutch, but Quayesha's the only one with a cell phone, and she can't get a signal this far underground.

"How'd you know?" I ask.

Nate just laughs and brushes a bit of dirt off his shoulder. "There's not much I don't know, kid—especially when it comes to magic. Now, I get that you want to be a good friend to your boy Vik, but hiding a phoenix ain't easy . . . and packing that kind of heat could attract the wrong sort of people, if you know what I mean."

I hadn't thought about that. Vik gave me the egg so I could keep it safe. "Do you think Blue will try to steal it?" I ask anxiously.

"Hard to say," Nate replies. "He's got other priorities right now, but it's still a risky proposition. Newborns are a lot of work—look at all the trouble those baby dragons caused! You're playing with fire, kid. Literally."

"I wish Trub was here," I say dejectedly.

Nate puts his tiny paw on my knee. "If there's one thing I know about you, Jax, it's that you're good at finding allies. You found them here in Brooklyn, and you'll find them in Chi-Town. Me? I trust my nose. It never lets me down. You ain't a rat like me, so you gotta trust your gut. Deep down you'll know when you've found a true friend."

I jump when I hear Quayesha shouting into her phone.

"Dutch! It's Quay. Can you hear me? Dutch?"

Nate pats my knee and says, "Time to go. Think about what I said, kid. Trub'll join you as soon as he can. Till then, just lay low and try to act natural. If you keep your hand in your pocket all day, folks are gonna know you got something valuable in there. Good luck!"

"Thanks, Nate."

He scampers into the shadows, and I rejoin the others.

Ma looks annoyed. "So much for technology. We may have to make other plans, ladies. Dutch should've been here by now."

Quayesha slips her phone into the snakeskin purse that matches her boots. She doesn't seem as worried as the older witches. "Maybe she's having technical trouble. The UR hasn't been used since last year."

Mrs. Benjamin frowns. "It's her job to keep everything in working order. We were supposed to leave half an hour ago."

"Hush!" Ma says suddenly. "I think I hear the UR coming now."

We fall silent and strain to hear the sound of an approaching vehicle. I'm not sure if I should be listening for a train. There aren't any tracks on the ground. The walls of the cavern are made of packed dirt. Worms and moles can move through dirt, but what kind of magical contraption could carry five people hundreds of miles underground?

"There she is!" Quayesha cries excitedly.

We all turn to look in the direction she's pointing. In the distance, a bright light shines in the darkness, but whatever it's attached to seems to be moving slowly.

Then we hear a strange burping sound, and the light hurtles toward us. Ma lowers her cane in front of me, and the large glowing tube stutters to a stop just inches away.

It looks sort of like those long bubbles you can make if you have a wand to dip in a tray of soapy water. We made our own wands in science class last year—all we needed was two straws and two strings. The bubbles

we made were superlong, but they didn't stay afloat and popped easily.

I want to ask how we're going to travel underground in *that* but figure it's probably a good idea not to ask any more questions for a while.

"Let's get on board," Ma says.

I stand back and watch as Quayesha grabs her suitcase and walks straight into the UR—right through the shimmering wall, or skin, or whatever it is. Mrs. Benjamin does the same, and I wait for Ma to go next, but she nods for me to go instead. I take a deep breath and walk through what feels like a spiderweb. Something slight and sticky tugs at my face and body, but before I can react, I'm inside the UR. Ma pushes me forward with her cane and points to a rack at one end of the glassy tube.

"Leave the suitcase over there and take a seat, Jax."

"Sorry for the delay, y'all," says a big woman with freckles and a gap between her front teeth. She's seated at the front of the tube, so this must be our conductor, Dutch.

She looks puzzled. "Never had any trouble with the UR before."

Dutch is dressed in grease-stained denim coveralls and dusty work boots. Her bronze cornrows are partly covered by an engineer's cap that's pulled down low over her green eyes. "Let's just get this show on the road," she says impatiently.

"Good idea," Ma says, settling beside me on one of two cushioned benches. There's a table in the middle that separates us from the other two witches. Dutch is up front on an elevated chair that swivels.

"And for the record," Ma continues, "nobody's blaming you, Dutch. The guardhouse misfired last time I used it to cross over. That fool Blue's upset the natural order of things. I'm not one bit surprised that the UR's acting up, too."

I decide I'd better tell Ma what Nate revealed. "Nate stopped by with a message. Trub isn't coming, and . . . Blue has already left Brooklyn."

"To spread his mischief, no doubt," Mrs. Benjamin says.

"Nothing we can do about it down here," Ma says. "Let's get going, Dutch."

Dutch turns to face the darkness that lies ahead of the tube. "I think we're in for a bumpy ride, so buckle up," she advises us.

I put on my own seat belt and then help Ma stretch hers over her puffy coat. Dutch grips a lever next to her seat and strains to push it forward. The tube begins burrowing into the earth around us. Over her shoulder, Dutch explains, "The UR is meant to operate like a pneumatic tube, so it should feel like being launched out of a slingshot or sucked into the hose of a vacuum cleaner. Fast and smooth."

The UR stalls and then lurches ahead. Dutch curses under her breath and says, "Wish I knew why it keeps hiccuping like that."

Hiccups are annoying but harmless. What's happening to the UR feels more like a heart attack! I'm grateful we're strapped into our seats. I'd rather not think about it but have to consider the possibility that *I* am the problem—or rather, the phoenix egg in my pocket is. If the UR always ran smoothly before, then maybe the others also suspect that I'm to blame.

We're sitting so close together that it feels like all eyes are on me. Even though the UR is transparent from the outside, from within there's no view out the window, just a reflection of the train's interior. I glance at Ma, Mrs. Benjamin, and Quayesha, but they're busy talking to each other. Maybe I'm just being paranoid.

Mrs. Benjamin pulls a cardboard box out of her bag. It's got grease stains on it, and the smell that fills the UR tells me there's food inside.

Ma turns to me and asks, "Ready for lunch?"

I feel like I ate breakfast not too long ago, so I shake my head and say, "No, thanks."

"Suit yourself," Ma replies before digging in her own purse to pull out a clear plastic container. Inside is what looks like potato salad.

Ma likes to eat, but I've never seen her cook, so I'm not sure where the potato salad came from. I didn't know I was supposed to bring something to share and wish I'd brought along a couple of bottles of root beer from Ma's fridge.

Quayesha digs in her purse until she finds a bottle of

hot sauce. She sets it on the table and then looks from Ma to Mrs. Benjamin. "What?"

"That's all you brought?" Mrs. Benjamin asks indignantly.

Quayesha folds her arms across her chest and says, "Now, you know no road trip would be complete without my world-famous pound cake. I was just saving space on the table for your fried chicken and side dishes, Mrs. B. Come on, y'all, let's eat! I'm starving."

Mrs. Benjamin takes a folded square of red-checkered fabric out of her bag along with some real cutlery. Ma spreads the cloth over the table, and Quayesha lays out the knives and forks. Mrs. Benjamin adds some kind of greens to the menu along with rice and peas and glistening chunks of sweet fried plantains. Before long, Dutch swivels around in her chair and accepts the plate Ma has fixed for her.

The food must taste as good as it smells, because for a while there's no talking inside the UR. I don't know how they can even think about eating when the elastic tube we're in keeps lurching forward, then stopping and starting again, like a Slinky going down a flight of stairs. I feel my heavy breakfast churning in my belly, and hope I don't heave it up onto Mrs. Benjamin's nice tablecloth. It's clear she doesn't like me, and I've already seen her eyes lingering on my travel clothes. Does she have X-ray vision? I think about what Nate said and try to keep my hand away from my pocket.

When the UR comes to a stop and doesn't start again, Dutch turns back around and tries shifting gears in an attempt to solve the problem. Finally, she gets us moving again and settles in to finish eating her meal. The look on Dutch's face tells me that she's still puzzling over the UR.

"Think there's a gremlin in the engine?" Ma asks before biting into a thick wedge of golden pound cake.

At first, I think Ma's joking, but then I realize she's not. I can't even see an engine anywhere in the UR and hope I don't see a gremlin, either!

Dutch bites into a chicken leg and chews on her food and her thoughts for a while. "Can't say. Had no trouble at all till I got near the park."

"Could be excess weight," Quayesha suggests, using one of her long nails to free something stuck in her teeth. "Not that Jax weighs all that much," she adds with a wink.

I smile nervously and go back to staring at the red and white squares on the tablecloth.

Mrs. Benjamin dabs at her own mouth with a paper

napkin before remarking, "We've all ridden the UR before without incident. Except for the boy, of course."

I glance up and find her dark, piercing eyes on me. It's a relief when Quayesha breaks Mrs. Benjamin's gaze by holding out the grease-stained box so everyone can deposit their chicken bones and other trash.

Ma burps loudly and declares, "We should arrive in about twenty minutes, by my calculations. Thank you, ladies, for a lovely meal. I know we're here on business, but it's always a pleasure to travel with you."

"It is indeed," Mrs. Benjamin replies.

"Think I'll take a quick nap, if you don't mind," Ma says.

"Excellent idea," says Mrs. Benjamin.

"Think I'll join you, too," Dutch says with a loud yawn.

I hope the UR is on autopilot because before long Dutch starts to snore. Quayesha pokes my leg with the pointy toe of her boot and asks, "Know why the UR was created?"

I shake my head, and she leans across the table so I can hear her over the low rumble of the snoring witches.

"There are a couple of theories. Number one." Quayesha pauses to hold up one of her magnificently manicured nails. "Some folks think we call it the UR because it was the original mode of transportation for Black witches—dating back at least to the time of Tituba, and probably even earlier. With all that hysteria going on in Salem, weren't no way you'd catch one of us flying up in the sky on a broom!"

I've heard about the Salem witch trials, but I've never heard of Tituba. I doubt my phone will work underground, so I make a mental note to look that name up once we reach Chicago.

Quayesha holds up another finger and says, "Number two. Other folks think we call it the UR because segregation forced us underground. Back in the day, the Supreme Council started getting complaints from witches who weren't permitted to travel first class because of their race. Some chose to drive to the annual convention but that could be dangerous, too, even after the *Green Book* came out in the 1930s. You know about that, right?"

I do, but this time I'm careful not to show off. "It told Black people where they could eat and find a place to stay when they were driving across the country."

"That's right. Well, this one witch, Henrietta Worley, decided she'd had enough of mean ol' Jim Crow. So Hetty designed—or revived—a vehicle that could operate underground. It was fast, clean, and comfortable—a way for witches like us to travel in style. Finally, we had a place of our own where we could be ourselves and be safe."

"I know things were bad during the witch trials in Salem, but a lot has changed since the 1600s. Is it still dangerous to be a witch?" I ask.

Quayesha looks fondly at the women dozing around us and sighs. "Women like us always pay a price for having too much power. But when we're together like this—here in the UR and at the annual convention—I don't just feel accepted and protected. I feel free."

She pauses and shifts her gaze from the other witches back to me. "Is it dangerous to be a witch? Sometimes. We can't control everything that happens in the world around us, but we've all taken a vow to use the skills we have to help others. People need us, Jax, and that's what makes the risk worthwhile."

This is the first time I've heard anything about a vow. Ma's only taught me two rules, and I doubt I could help anybody with the little I've learned so far. "I want to learn how to help people, but . . ." I glance over at Ma and lower my voice, even though she's asleep. "Ma keeps saying I'm not ready."

"She would know, right? Ma's been a witch longer than anyone else I know," Quayesha says with obvious admiration. "She talks about you all the time, Jax."

"Really?"

"Really. We were all surprised when Ma said she was taking on a new apprentice. At her age, Ma could have just eased into retirement without the bother of training someone new. But she didn't, which tells me she sees something special in you, Jax. Ma won't give you any more or less than you can handle. I know it's hard to wait when you feel ready to learn, but try to be patient with her. Think you can do that?"

I nod at Quayesha and make a silent apprentice's vow of my own.

5

"Welcome to the South Side of Chicago," Ma says with a smile.

This time there are no paving stones that form a staircase. Instead, we take turns squeezing into a narrow elevator that opens in the base of a monument at the corner of a busy intersection. Ma hustles me out of the tight box and onto the street so the elevator can go back underground to pick up the other witches. I turn around, look up, and see a statue of George Washington on a horse with his sword raised above his head. Someone has tagged the granite base with red spray paint. Someone else has tried to scrub the words away.

Quayesha and Mrs. Benjamin come up next, followed by Dutch. The sun is shining in a cloudless blue sky, but the leaves on the trees have already started to change colors. It feels like autumn has arrived here, too, and I can see why they call it the Windy City. Gusts send crisp leaves scraping along the sidewalk, and I shiver despite my warm hoodie. The bright sunlight makes me squint, but I still see a few white flakes floating by.

Before I can ask if it's snowing in Chicago, Ma sees them, too, and says, "Looks like Blue's been busy."

Mrs. Benjamin sucks her teeth in disgust, but Quayesha doesn't seem fazed. She shakes a few flakes out of her locks and says, "It's just one more thing he'll have to answer for."

"True," Ma says grudgingly. Then she points up a wide boulevard that's named after Martin Luther King Jr. "We're heading this way."

We follow Ma up the tree-lined street until we reach a huge house behind a tall cast-iron fence. Ma says, "This is where we're staying. Let's drop off our bags and clean up before we head to the convention."

Dutch clears her throat and nods her head in my direction, though she's looking at Ma. "You sure Missy won't have a problem with Junior?"

Dutch keeps calling me that for some reason, but I decide not to bother correcting her.

Ma says, "Don't you worry 'bout the boy. He's my responsibility, not yours."

Dutch shrugs and gives me a sad sort of half grin,

which makes me wonder what this Missy has against kids like me. We follow Ma across the street. There are no brownstones like back home in Brooklyn. Instead, the block is filled with big gray stone houses that look a bit like castles. The one we'll be staying in even has two turrets! There's a stone balcony on the third floor. Beneath it a bunch of strange symbols are carved into the stone panels that frame a beautiful stained glass window. The midday sun picks up the rich blues and greens of a peacock's fanned feathers.

Quayesha leans in and whispers, "Nice, right? You should see it from the inside. That room's right under the ballroom."

Ballroom? When Ma said we'd be staying in a rooming house, I thought it would be shabby compared to a hotel, but I was totally wrong. At the side of the building there's a long pond with lily pads and purple lotuses floating on the surface of the water. I don't see a fountain, but I can hear the soft murmur of falling water, and the scales of golden carp flash in the sunlight as they swim around the pond.

Ma opens the cast-iron gate, and that's when I see the sign on the lawn: MISS ELLABELLE'S HOME FOR WORKING WOMEN AND GIRLS. Dutch glances at me again, and I figure maybe I should be the one to speak up this time.

"Um . . . are boys allowed to stay here, too?" I ask Ma.

She just shushes me as a tiny woman wearing horn-rimmed glasses opens one of the wide wooden doors and steps out onto the porch. The pearls around her brown neck gleam in the flickering light cast by the large lantern hanging above her head. Our host looks even more unpleasant than the two sneering gargoyles that cling to the grapevines carved into the stone columns.

"Ma," she says with a slight nod but no smile.

It's not the warmest welcome, but Ma grins just the same and offers her own hand in greeting. The woman barely touches the tips of Ma's fingers before folding her arms across her pearl-buttoned pink cardigan.

"Afternoon, Miss Ellabelle. You sure are a sight for sore eyes. We've had quite a journey—the UR was acting up, so we're a little worse for wear." Ma chuckles and pats her Afro, which isn't messy at all but still looks a bit wild next to our host's tight silver bun.

Miss Ellabelle glares at me over the top of her glasses. I'm tempted to shift so that I'm hidden by Ma's puffy coat, but I haven't done anything wrong, so why should I hide? Plus, it's the twenty-first century! I'm pretty sure it's illegal to deny someone a place to stay just because they're not a girl. Also, Ma's a witch. Surely this unpleasant little woman won't try to tell my boss what she can and can't do.

Ma tries again. "How long has it been since I was a guest here? Ten or twelve years?"

"Too long, apparently. Need I remind you, Ma, that there are certain rules that must be followed if you are to stay at this establishment?"

"Of course, Miss E. It's just that Jaxon is my apprentice, and since this is his first time visiting Chicago, I wanted him to experience the finest accommodation. But if you're willing to issue us a refund, I suppose we could try to find another play to stay. . . ." Ma turns to Mrs. Benjamin and asks, "Doesn't Clara Simpson run a bed-and-breakfast nearby?"

"It's just one block over, I believe," Mrs. Benjamin replies with a straight face, though Dutch smirks and Quayesha smothers a snicker.

Miss Ellabelle must not want to lose paying guests to her neighbor, because she sniffs and says, "Well, I suppose I can make an exception just this once. He does appear to be clean, at least."

Ma's determined to be polite, but the smile on her face is slipping. "Jaxon is very tidy and very polite. He'll be no trouble at all, I can assure you," Ma says in a terse voice. "Now if you don't mind showing us to our rooms, we'll just leave our bags and make our way to the convention."

Miss Ellabelle finally steps aside, and Ma nods at the snooty little woman as she leads the rest of us up the stone stairs and into the impressive foyer. A chandelier hangs from the high ceiling, and portraits of elegantly dressed people hang on the walls. The wallpaper looks like it's made of gold and red velvet, but I don't dare touch it with my fingers. To the right is a dining room with dark green walls and a long table that could seat at least twenty guests. To the left is the parlor. The pocket doors are only partially open, but I glimpse a grand piano in one corner, a fireplace that I could almost stand inside, and old-fashioned sofas covered in protective plastic.

Miss Ellabelle sees me craning my neck to get a better look and pulls the doors shut.

"The parlor is off-limits," she says.

Ma raises an eyebrow, which makes me wonder if our host is making up new rules just for me.

"Your rooming house looks more like a castle," I tell Miss Ellabelle, hoping my attempt at flattery will work as well as Ma's.

But our unhappy host just scowls at me and says, "It was patterned after the sixteenth-century château of the king of France." Then she points to a rubber boot tray and says, "Shoes."

I kneel to remove my sneakers, and the others slip their shoes off as well. In our sock feet we pad up the carpeted stairs, the curved wooden staircase creaking beneath our weight.

I hang back a bit to put more space between myself and Miss Ellabelle. She's talking about the history of the building. It's clear she's very proud to be carrying on the tradition of her grandmother, who was born enslaved in Missouri but came to Chicago and opened a home in the 1920s for the many migrant women who flocked to the city looking for jobs.

I look up and see the head of a bison mounted on the wall. Then my mouth falls open because the shaggy head turns to look down at me before pulling its head out of the wall with a soft popping sound! Only a wood plaque with a gaping hole remains on the wall.

No one else seems to have witnessed the bison's vanishing act. I tug Quayesha's hand to get her attention. "Is Miss Ellabelle . . . a hunter?"

Quayesha shakes her head and says, "I think her grandmother bought the house furnished, so that probably belonged to the original owner."

I glance up at the empty plaque and ask, "Is Miss Ellabelle a witch?" I can easily imagine our unpleasant host with a pointy black hat, stirring a cauldron full of green goop that turns boys like me into toads!

But Quayesha just laughs. "There's magic somewhere in her family, which is why she rents rooms to folks like us. But there is nothing remotely magical about Miss E. She chose another path that's *very* straight and *very* narrow."

I look up to find Miss Ellabelle glaring at me from the second-floor landing. There are more questions I'd like to ask Quayesha, but I zip my lip and hurry up the stairs to join the rest of our group.

Our host explains that we'll have the entire second floor to ourselves for the next three days. I wait my turn as Miss Ellabelle leads us down the long hallway, stopping to open a door and deposit a witch in one grand bedroom after another. Some have four-poster beds with velvet canopies; others have crystal chandeliers and marble fireplaces. When we get to the end of the hall, there's only one door left.

"And this," she says with obvious pleasure, "is your room, boy."

Miss Ellabelle turns the knob and steps aside so I can see where I'll be sleeping. There's an old cot folded up at the far end of the room and a strange square door in the middle of the water-stained wall. There are dusty marks on the wall where shelves once hung, and the narrowness of the room tells me it probably used to be a storage closet.

I don't want to seem rude, but in a big, fancy house like this, why should I have to sleep in a musty storeroom? Then I think maybe this is how all apprentices are treated—just like how servants used to have to sleep way up in the attic of the big houses where they worked. Ma looks at my face and generously offers to share her room with me.

"That's okay," I tell her, trying to be a good sport. "I don't need much space." What I do need is a little privacy. This room may not have any windows and may smell faintly like mothballs, but it's mine.

"All right, folks!" Ma calls so the others can hear her. "Let's meet back downstairs in five minutes."

I take my phone out so I can charge the battery, only to find there's no plug in my room. "It's definitely a closet," I mutter to myself before texting Mama to let her know we arrived safely. I consider sending her a photo of my room, but that would only make her worry.

I check the time before putting my phone away. We're in the central time zone now, so we've actually gained an hour. Since I don't have much to unpack, I head downstairs, pausing to take a closer look at the wooden plaque on which the bison's head was mounted.

"Come on, boy, don't dillydally!"

I hurry down the curved staircase and find Ma at the bottom, wearing the same clothes she had on before.

"What you staring at, boy?" Ma asks grumpily.

"Aren't you going to get changed?" I ask.

Ma scowls at me. "You saying there's something wrong with the clothes I got on?"

I shake my head. "No! I just thought . . . I don't know. I didn't think witches could wear everyday clothes to a convention."

Quayesha laughs and picks a ball of lint off her sparkly pink T-shirt. She has swapped her dress and boots for skinny jeans and a pair of leopard-print high-top sneakers. "There's a gala on the last night. We'll wear our fancy clothes then. Hope you packed your tuxedo, Jax."

Mrs. Benjamin sighs impatiently and nudges Ma

through the open front door and down the stairs. The rest of us follow, but when we reach the street, Ma puts her hand on my shoulder and says, "All right, Jax. Vonn should be here soon."

"Who's Vonn?" I ask.

"Only the best tour guide in all of Chicago," Quayesha says with a smile.

Tour guide? I turn back to Ma. "I thought I was going to the convention with you."

"Not today," Ma says without looking me in the eye.

"But . . . what if you need help?"

Mrs. Benjamin snorts and starts heading up the block. Ma doesn't mean to hurt my feelings, but she can tell how disappointed I am. Why bring me all the way to Chicago if I'm not allowed to learn about the world of witches?

"We'll be stuck in meetings all day long, Jax," Ma explains. "You'll have a lot more fun with Vonn."

"I didn't come to Chicago to have fun, Ma. I came to learn."

"I know, boy, but you got to trust me on this. We got some serious matters to discuss at the convention, and I'm afraid you just ain't ready to join the conversation."

"Can I go with you tomorrow? I promise not to say a single word—I'll just listen."

Ma sighs impatiently, and I know that's my cue to stop begging. I try not to look as frustrated as I feel and take a seat on the bottom step of the stoop.

"You got pocket money?" she asks before following after the others.

"Yes, ma'am," I mutter as I wave goodbye. Mama gave me some money for emergencies. I'm pretty sure that, like me, she thought I'd be with Ma all the time and wouldn't have to worry about buying my own meals. Then I remember the way they were whispering in the kitchen last night. Was Mama telling Ma *not* to take me to the convention? Maybe this Vonn is just a glorified babysitter.

I sigh and get ready to throw myself a pity party. Like the porch columns, the stone banisters on either side of the stairs are covered with strange carvings. I peer at the one closest to me and see that what I thought was a large flower is actually a face. I do a double take when a pair of stone eyes opens and looks me up and down. Then the face yawns, and its eyes close once more.

"I know how you feel," I say. "I didn't expect Chicago to be this boring, either."

Then I see a teenager loping up the block. Judging from his clothes and the too-cool-for-school way he moves, he's the kind of kid who'd never be caught dead with a nerd like me. But to my surprise, he nods his baseball-capped head at me before jogging across the street. The logo on the teen's cap matches the one on the sleeve of his white pin-striped jersey. CHICAGO is spelled out across his chest in navy-blue letters. I'm not sure I've ever seen sneakers so clean—they must be brand-new, because there's not a single scuff mark on his white kicks. When he pulls open the gate, I see my own reflection in the mirrored lenses of his sunglasses

and wish I had a pair of my own to block the glare of his all-white ensemble.

"What up, Brooklyn?"

He holds his hand out and I reach for it, hoping my handshake has enough steps.

After three variations, Vonn pulls me up off the bottom step and looks me over for a few seconds. Then he asks, "Mets or Yankees?"

"Uh . . ."

Before I can think of an answer, Vonn fires off another question. "Jets or Giants?"

"Well . . ."

"Rangers or Isles? Knicks or Nets?"

Finally I say, "My dad took me to Madison Square Garden to see the Liberty play once."

"Yeah? A buddy of mine works at the arena. Maybe he can score us some tickets to see the Sky play."

I hope I look sufficiently impressed. The truth is, I'm not really into sports. My dad was a sports journalist and always hoped I'd share his love of basketball, but when it became clear that I didn't have the hand-eye coordination it takes to dribble or hit a free throw, Dad found other things for us to do together. I don't tell Vonn that at that Liberty game I ate so many hot dogs that I fell asleep long before the game ended.

I can't think of anything else to say about sports teams, so I focus on Vonn's jersey. "What team is that?" I ask, pointing to the logo on his sleeve.

"The Chicago American Giants," he says while tracing the A that's laid over the letter G. "They dominated the Negro Leagues back in the day."

I've seen the word *Negro* in my history textbook, but nowadays we call ourselves Black or African American. I wonder how a kid his age knows about sports teams that played such a long time ago. "Do you play baseball?"

"Nope. You hungry?"

My stomach settled down once we got off the UR and does feel a little empty right now. "I guess. I have a granola bar in my bag."

Vonn grins, and I blink as the diamond grillz on his front teeth glitter. "Save your snack for later, Brooklyn. What you need is a real meal. Deep-dish or thin-crust?"

Deep-dish pizza sounds a lot better than a dry granola bar! Mama is lactose intolerant and so am I, but I can't come all the way to Chicago and not try the city's famous pizza. Maybe spending the day with Vonn won't be so bad after all.

"So, Brooklyn, what you know 'bout the Chi?"

I shrug. "Not a lot. My dad used to come here for work. He sent me a postcard once of the big silver bean."

"Cloud Gate. That's in Millennium Park. Did your pops tell you anything 'bout the South Side?"

When I shake my head, Vonn spreads out his arms before turning in a circle once. "This is Bronzeville. They used to call this part of Chicago 'Black Metropolis,' but Bronzeville is the name that stuck. The fearless journalist Ida B. Wells lived a few blocks north along King Drive. Great writers like Richard Wright and Gwendolyn Brooks lived here, too, along with jazz legends like Nat King Cole and Louis Armstrong."

"I thought Louis Armstrong lived in Queens," I say.

"That's where he ended up," Vonn explains. "A lot of musicians made their way to New York eventually, but Satchmo got his start here in Chicago with King Oliver's band. You like jazz?"

I shrug. "When he's home, my granddad plays scratchy old records. Some of the music is okay."

"Trub's your granddaddy, right?"

I nod and feel proud that Vonn knows something about my family. "He was supposed to come with us, but . . ."

"Plans change—that's just how it is. You gotta learn how to go with the flow. I know this ain't how you thought you'd be spending your first day in Chicago, but it looks like we're stuck with each other, so we might as well make the best of it. You feel me?"

I laugh and say, "I feel you, Vonn."

"Right. You want deep-dish. Should we go to Giordano's or Lou Malnati's?"

"You choose. I'm just going with the flow," I say with a smile.

Vonn laughs. "Let's hit Giordano's over in Hyde Park. You good to walk awhile? If not, we can wait for the 15 bus."

"I like to walk," I tell him. "My dad always said that was the best way to get to know a new place."

"Couldn't agree more. Let's go, Brooklyn."

Vonn loops his arm around my neck, and we walk like that for a long while, stopping now and then so he can point out a landmark or tell me a story about someone famous who lived in the neighborhood—including the Obamas! Many of the people we pass seem to know Vonn, and he shakes a lot of hands as we walk. Some older women smile at us like they're pleased—or maybe proud—to see us hanging out together. I wonder if they think Vonn's my big brother. I'm learning so much from him, I almost wish he was!

We walk for close to an hour, but I'm still surprised

when I look up and see the bright lights of the Giordano's sign up ahead.

"We're here, at last. Ready to get your eat on?" Vonn asks.

I nod eagerly and pass through the door he holds open for me. Inside the restaurant is busy and loud. Most tables are taken, and there are a few people in line ahead of us. But when the manager sees Vonn, he opens his arms wide and gives both of us a big hug. Then he leads us to a more private table in a corner of the restaurant and asks, "The usual, my friend?"

Vonn nods and asks me what I want to drink.

"I'll have a beer," I say, trying not to smirk.

Vonn just chuckles and asks the manager to bring us two root beers and some garlic fries. "Deep-dish pizza takes a long time, but it's totally worth the wait," Vonn assures me.

I wonder if President Obama and his family ever come here for deep-dish. I'm about to ask Vonn, when his phone dings and he starts texting somebody. I watch the other diners in the restaurant. If people know about the strange sleep illness spreading across the city, they sure don't look worried. But then, most of the diners are young, and Ma thinks the spell only affects older folks.

The waiter brings our drinks and appetizer. I get my reusable straw out of my bag and quickly drain about a third of my soda. Vonn slips his phone back into his pocket and takes just one small sip of his root beer. I can't see his eyes, but his face looks different—more tense than before.

"Everything okay?" I ask.

Vonn nods and takes his grillz out before grabbing a handful of garlic fries. "Just some business I gotta take care of later on."

I sip my root beer more slowly and try to decide whether it's a good idea to ask Vonn a personal question.

Vonn laughs and says, "Don't ever play poker, kid. I can read you like a book. What's on your mind?"

"I was just wondering . . . I mean, are you . . . um . . . how do you know Ma?"

"Me and Ma go way back. In fact, I've known her since she was round about your age."

My mouth falls open, and my straw clanks against the glass mug. "But . . . I thought you were a teenager!"

Vonn smiles, and his own teeth are just as bright as his white clothes. "Black don't crack, baby."

"So . . . if you're older than Ma, does that mean . . . are you also . . ."

Vonn leans in and whispers, "A witch?"

I nod, and he pushes back from the table. "Naw. I'm a Watcher." Vonn slides his sunglasses down his nose just enough for me to see his eyes. They're dark brown, like mine, but in the center of each one, instead of a black pupil, there's an orange light.

The waiter returns to drop off some plates and napkins, so Vonn slides his shades back into place. When we're alone again he asks, "Anything else you wanna know?"

A dozen questions swirl around my mind, but I settle on the most obvious one. "What's a Watcher?"

6

The waiter sets our steaming-hot pizza on the table between us. The tomato sauce looks strange on top, but I see all the layers of meat and cheese stacked beneath it when the waiter serves each of us a big slice. I wait to see if Vonn's going to eat with his hands and sigh with relief when he reaches for his cutlery instead.

"Deep-dish can get pretty messy," he tells me as he tucks his paper napkin into the neck of his vintage baseball jersey. "Don't wanna get any sauce on my gear," Vonn explains as he smooths down his clean white bib.

I do the same with my napkin, and soon there's silence at our table as we chew on mouthfuls of cheesy, sausage-filled pizza.

Vonn finishes his slice first and just watches me for a while. He grins and says, "It's good, right?"

It takes a minute for me to swallow. "It's amazing. Thanks for bringing me here, Vonn."

"Ma would never forgive me if I didn't show you a good time on your first day in the Windy City," he replies.

Vonn reaches for a second slice of pizza, and I try to steer the conversation back to his job title.

"So . . . how long have you been a Watcher?"

Vonn laughs and says, "I got here just a few weeks after DuSable. You know 'bout that brother, right?"

"DuSable? That sounds French," I say.

"Good ear, Brooklyn. Jean Baptiste Point DuSable. Black man, born in Haiti, educated in France. Sailed to New Orleans and then came up the Mississippi and was the first non-Native settler to set up shop right here on the Chicago River. Before DuSable arrived, this land belonged to the Council of the Three Fires: the Ojibwe, Odawa, and Bodewadmi Nations. The Ojibwe are keepers of the Faith, the Odawa are keepers of the Trade, and the Bodewadmi are the home keepers of the Fire. They had neighbors, of course—the Miami, Ho-Chunk, Menominee, Sac, and Fox.

"Now, DuSable, he married a Bodewadmi woman named Kitihawa, had a coupla kids. Opened a trading post, ran a farm, built a real nice house for his family.

My man spoke five, six languages. DuSable was the real deal."

For a moment I feel bad about the way I judged Vonn when I first saw him walking up the block. Vonn really is the best tour guide ever. I never imagined that someone who looked like a blinged-out teenage rapper could be so knowledgeable.

"When did DuSable settle here?" I ask.

Vonn smiles and says, "In 1779."

My eyes pop as I do the math. Vonn puts another forkful of pizza into his mouth, which gives me time to think about my next question. "Why did you choose Chicago—or were you sent here?"

"It didn't take DuSable long to figure out what the Native Americans knew all along—where rivers meet, people meet, too. This has been a gathering place for centuries. And when people from different places get together . . . magic happens. My job is to wait and watch."

I'm a little disappointed by Vonn's response. Being a Watcher sounds pretty straightforward—boring, even. "Do you work for anyone?" I expect him to say "Sis," but Vonn surprises me.

After lifting the corner of his napkin to wipe some tomato sauce from his mouth, he says, "I'm more of a freelancer, actually. I watch people, places, events. Ma asked me to watch *you* for a few days, so here I am."

"She doesn't want me at the convention." Saying that out loud to someone as cool as Vonn makes me feel even worse. I keep my eyes on my plate until Vonn nudges my foot with his pristine white sneaker.

"I'm sure Ma has her reasons. And it ain't that bad hanging out with me, is it?"

I smile and shake my head. Vonn puts another slice of pizza on my plate. "Can I ask *you* a question?"

"Sure," I say, but then fill my mouth with another delicious bite.

"Ma tells me you offered to be her apprentice—even though she's about to retire. Why?"

Chewing all that mozzarella gives me time to think about my response. Why *do* I want to be Ma's apprentice?

"Did Ma tell you about the three dragons?"

Vonn nods, so I go on.

"I guess . . . I just want to be useful—to help Ma help others. But I can't do that if she won't show me how."

Vonn leans back and folds his arms across his chest. "You got friends, right? And family?"

"Sure," I reply.

"I bet you help them out all the time."

I nod and feel the weight of the phoenix egg in my pocket.

"Ma's got special skills—no doubt about it—and I bet she'll share them with you when you're ready. But for now, don't focus on what you *don't* know. If you wanna help folks, just do it. You don't need magic for that." Vonn leans forward to finish his slice. "Am I right?" he asks before taking another bite.

"I guess. It's just that I worked hard to prove myself to Ma. We've been through a lot together, and I thought she really believed I'd make a good apprentice. But now she acts like she's changed her mind about me, and I don't know why."

"Have you asked her?"

I shake my head, expecting Vonn to say something about the importance of letting folks know how you feel. After all, Ma can't read my mind—can she? That thought makes me nervously clutch the buzzing egg. Why should I expect Ma to trust me when I'm the one keeping secrets?

I glance at Vonn and see my own uncertain face reflected in his sunglasses. Should I tell him about the phoenix? I bet Vonn could give me some good advice on what to do. Just as I open my mouth to tell him the truth,

Vonn claps his hands and then rubs them together. The diamonds on his chunky rings flash in the sun.

"A'ight, Brooklyn. We've got the rest of the afternoon to explore the city. Where you wanna go next?"

I shrug and rub my stomach. I ate way too much pizza, and my belly feels like it's about to explode. Vonn smiles and says, "Maybe we should walk for a little while. Give your gut a chance to settle down."

I nod and follow him out of the restaurant and across the street. The sun is out and the sky is blue, but a cool wind ruffles the crisp leaves already covering the sidewalk.

"This here's the Midway," Vonn says after we've been walking awhile. "You been to Central Park, right?"

"Sure, though I mostly go to Prospect Park, since that's in Brooklyn."

"Same two dudes designed all of 'em: Olmsted and Vaux. You ever been up on a Ferris wheel?"

"My dad took me on the one at Coney Island," I tell him.

"The first amusement park at Coney Island was basically a copy of the one they put up here on the Midway for the World's Fair back in 1893."

"Cool," I say as I gaze over at the grassy valley on our right.

"The World's Fair was a big deal, with close to fifty countries sending people to show off what they were building and inventing and eating and stuff like that."

"Were Black people allowed to go? I mean, was the fair segregated?"

Vonn waggles his hand, which means "sort of," I think.

"Yes and no. Remember—it was 1893. When was slavery abolished?"

I don't have to think too long to come up with the answer. Slavery ended when the North won the Civil War. "In 1865 with the passage of the Thirteenth Amendment."

"That's right. So most Black folks hadn't even been free for thirty years! But we'd come a long way in that time, and a few folks decided to set the record straight. Remember Ida B. Wells?"

"The journalist who lived in Bronzeville?"

"That's right. Well, she and her husband and my boy Freddie Douglass printed a pamphlet that told the truth about African Americans and their contributions to this country. With a little help, they handed it out to thousands of guests."

I frown. "We always have to fight to be included. It's not fair."

"True. But when you want something real bad, you

learn to fight for it. And that makes you stronger," Vonn says.

"It makes you tired, too," I reply, stomping on a crisp brown leaf. "And mad."

Vonn nods. "Check it out—there was a debate at the World's Fair. Should African Americans go back to the Motherland, or should we stay here in the US? A lot of Black folks felt like we'd never be accepted or treated fairly here. Some felt we didn't belong here because our roots were in Africa. Other folks, like Freddie D., argued that America was the only home most of us had ever known. We didn't come here by choice like other immigrants, but it was our blood, sweat, and tears that built this country. Like it or not, we're African *and* American. What do you think?"

I want to visit Africa someday. Mama took a DNA test and discovered our ancestors came from Nigeria and Cameroon. We don't know their names, but it would still be kind of cool to go across the ocean and learn more about those countries. Would I feel at home in Nigeria? I don't know. Would I fit in because I'm Black, or would I stand out because I'm American?

Suddenly, I think about Mo and wonder how the dragon Kavita stole is doing now that it's in the realm of magic. The little dragon must be glad to be reunited with its siblings, but maybe it misses Brooklyn, too. I'd miss the city if someone suddenly snatched me away.

Vonn brings my attention back to his tour. "The Midway connects Washington Park to Jackson Park. The DuSable Museum is back that way," Vonn says, jabbing his thumb over his shoulder. "It's closed right now, but maybe we can check that out tomorrow. This here on your left is the University of Chicago."

I look up at the impressive gray buildings rising above the tree line. They look like castles—I can even see gargoyles!

"Gothic—that's what that style of architecture's called," Vonn tells me.

"Are you a student here?" I ask him.

Vonn laughs and says, "I'm a student of life."

As we pass a tower, its bell tolls three o'clock. Vonn leads me over to the grassy valley, where a group of summer-camp kids play on the steps of a giant monument. It's sort of like the one I saw yesterday, but the figure on this horse looks like a knight in armor. Taped to the statue's base are drawings of, and messages to, Breonna Taylor. Most look like they were made by teenagers. Some are really good, even though they've been tagged with silver spray paint. The smaller cards wave like flags in the breeze and were clearly made by the littlest kids. These haven't been vandalized, and I smile as I stoop to read one signed by a girl named Madeline:

BAC LIFS MATR
I LOVE YOU BREONA TALR

I wonder how much these little kids know about the Movement for Black Lives. Mama and I talk about it whenever there's another police shooting. We even went to a big rally at Grand Army Plaza, and to my surprise, some of my White classmates were there, too. I look at the flimsy card with its misspelled words written in crayon. Little kids understand love, but they don't know how to make sense of hate. Neither do I.

Vonn taps me on the shoulder and says, "A'ight, Brooklyn. I gotta bounce at four, so our next stop will have to be the last one on the tour today."

I stand up and follow Vonn out of the valley. We pass under a bridge and keep heading east. "Are we almost at the lake?" I ask.

"Pretty much," Vonn replies. "We're coming up on Jackson Park, and Lake Michigan is on the other side. The Obama Presidential Library is being built over there. And that," he says, pointing across a busy road to a big building with a dome and white pillars, "is the

Museum of Science and Industry. They built it for the World's Fair. Ready?"

That's Rule #1, but I have to hustle to keep up with Vonn as he dashes across the street. A few cars honk angrily, but that doesn't faze Vonn. He leads me across the grass to a path that takes us over a bridge. Now we're on an island in the middle of a small lake. A sign tells me we're heading toward the Garden of the Phoenix.

I take a deep breath and tighten my grip on the egg humming in my pocket. "Where are we going?" I ask, even though I know the answer. What I really want to know is whether Vonn has somehow figured out my secret. Why else would he bring me here?

"The city can get kind of hectic sometimes. It's good to have a place you can go where you can hear yourself think. Know what I mean?"

I nod and see a wooden structure up ahead that must be the entrance to the garden. It feels like a gateway, though I don't see any doors. To the right there's a loose cluster of tall silver petals arranged to look like a flower opening to the sun.

I point to it and ask, "What's that?"

"*Skylanding*—a sculpture by Yoko Ono," Vonn tells me. "You know who that is?"

I shake my head, and Vonn goes on. "She's a famous

Japanese artist—you should Google her sometime. There used to be a building over there—the Ho-o-Den. It was built for the World's Fair and showed what traditional buildings looked like over in Japan. Too bad some fools lit it up back in 1946."

Vonn shakes his head and sighs. "Chicago stays burning—there's the Great Fire of 1871, Red Summer of 1919. You got the uprising in '68, when they assassinated MLK, and now the city's burning again. . . . It's a'ight, though," he assures me. "The phoenix always rises from the ashes, right? Like Mama Maya taught us back in the day: and still we rise."

The egg jumps suddenly, and I see Vonn's gaze drop to my pocket, but he doesn't say anything. Instead, he leads me into the garden, and for a while we walk along the gravel path without saying much. The egg stops jerking but buzzes more loudly. If Vonn can hear it, he shows no curiosity about the source. I follow him over a steeply curved wooden bridge. There are lily pads in the water below, but I don't see any carp.

"That's the shortest bridge I've ever crossed," I say with a chuckle.

Vonn gives me a serious nod. "In Japanese gardens, bridges are symbolic. Even a short bridge signals that you've passed from one world to another."

I think about that for a while. This place is peaceful but a lot smaller than the Japanese garden in Brooklyn. When we pass a toro—a stone lantern—I find myself fighting the urge to reach inside and deposit the troublesome egg. Farther on I see a sign next to a patch of moss. It reads:

SHH, BABY MOSS
AT REST
DO NOT DISTURB

For just a moment I wonder if it might be best to leave the egg here. The baby phoenix could rest on a soft bed of moss and hatch to become someone else's responsibility. But I promised Vik I'd take care of the egg. "I won't let you down, Vik. I'll keep my promise," I say to myself. Then I jump because Vonn leans in close and whispers in my ear.

"Word is bond," he says before swerving around me and strolling out of the garden.

Vonn knows. He *has* to know. But how? And is he going to tell Ma—or does she already know, too?

As we pass through the gardens' gabled gate, a crow's sharp call disturbs the peace, and the egg in my pocket practically flies out of my pocket. I'm about to confess everything to Vonn and ask for his help with the phoenix, when he glances up at the crow in the tree and then down at his phone.

"Think you can find your way back?" he asks me.

I try not to sound as panicked as I feel. "Back . . . home? On my own?"

"Don't sweat it, Brooklyn. The city's a grid. Keep the lake on your right side—that's east. So long as you know where the lake is, you'll have no trouble figuring out which way's west, north, and south." I must look a little anxious because Vonn asks, "You good?"

94

I have the address of the rooming house written down in my notebook. I don't really feel like finding my way back by myself when I've only been in Chicago a couple of hours, but the phoenix egg seems like it's about to erupt, so maybe it's best if I'm on my own.

I nod and try to sound more confident than I feel. "I'm good, Vonn. Thanks for showing me around and teaching me so much about the city."

"We just scraped the surface, Brooklyn. I'll swing by early tomorrow morning for round two. Cool?"

"Cool," I say, even though the vibrating egg in my pocket is definitely heating up. Vonn tips his cap at me before disappearing into the park. I take a deep breath and clutch the egg in my pocket.

"Just hold on," I tell it. "I'll have to figure this out by myself."

7

I make my way back over the bridge and out of Jackson Park. Without Vonn to guide me, I decide against jaywalking and head for the nearest intersection so I can cross at the lights. "Keep the lake on your right." That's simple enough. I walk north for a while and then turn left—that means I'm heading west and leaving the lake behind. I'm on Fifty-Sixth Street now, and the rooming house is just north of Forty-Seventh. Less than ten blocks—that doesn't sound so bad.

I walk north for a while and pass Giordano's before turning left onto Hyde Park Boulevard. I'm not sure how far west I have to walk before I reach King Drive. My phone's battery is low, but I decide to check the map app anyway. It tells me I've got over two miles to go! Time passed quickly when Vonn was here to tell me all about the neighborhood. Now the city feels foreign and lonely.

I wish I could find President Obama's house, but I can't remember where it is, and it's not like he'd actually be at home. The weather is changing, and as the wind picks up, I feel grateful for the extra warmth the buzzing egg provides.

Flashing lights and the sound of sirens distract me for a moment. A few blocks away, an ambulance is pulled up to the curb, and a crowd has gathered on the sidewalk. As I get closer, I see several weary elders being helped off a bus. All are struggling to stay awake long enough to share their address with the younger passengers trying to help them. One man who looks a bit like Trub is seated on the curb snoring loudly as a young woman tries to rouse him. I wish I had some silver root to help them stay alert, but the only thing in my pockets right now is an antsy phoenix.

I decide to head north instead of west to avoid the drama up ahead, but soon find myself in unfamiliar territory. I try to remember the landmarks Vonn pointed out earlier but finally have to admit that I'm lost. I can't tell where the lake is anymore, and when I look at my phone's screen, the empty battery icon just blinks up at me. I slip the phone in my back pocket and cross the street, hoping I'm still heading in the right direction. Things look different now that the sky is starting to get dark. Ominous gray clouds blot out the sun, and I hear the distant rumble of thunder. I don't have an umbrella—I hope I don't get soaked before I figure out how to get home.

As I pass a corner store, an older Black man holding a weathered paper coffee cup speaks to me. "What you need, Youngblood?"

I swallow hard and try to keep the egg from jumping out of my pocket. I mean to ask for directions, but instead, I softly say, "Fire. I need a fire, sir."

The old man squints at me and leans in closer. "A fire? You cold, son?" He strokes his stubbly chin in a way that makes me think of my grandfather. "Can't say I blame you. Mother Nature don't know if she's coming or going these days. We got a fire going over there." He steps away from me and hollers at a man across the street. "Joe! Hey, Joe! JOE!"

Annoyed, the man dumps the loose change from his cup into his coat pocket. Then he puts his hand on my shoulder and steers me across the street to an empty lot that looks more like a junkyard. Different car parts litter the ground, and tires are neatly stacked in one corner, hubcaps in another. Another man is standing by a rusted steel drum, his hands held up to the crackling flames inside.

"You ain't hear me calling your name, man?"

Joe, a tall man wrapped in a dingy Chicago Bears blanket, lifts one flap of his matching blue-and-orange trapper hat. "What's that, Frank?"

Frank just shakes his head and pulls me closer to the drum. "This young man needs warming up. I told him he could share our fire."

Joe sizes me up before asking, "Got any food, kid?"

For just a moment I wish I had the bag of marshmallows in the locked cupboard above Ma's fridge. But I'm far from Brooklyn, and we aren't at summer camp. I've got a job to do.

I slip my knapsack off and pull a granola bar out of the side pocket. I offer it to Joe, and he takes it with a nod of thanks. Then he opens the package, breaks the bar into three even pieces, and hands one to each of us. We munch in silence for a little while as the sky darkens. The rain hasn't started to fall yet, but the clouds above us are swirling in a way that makes me nervous.

Now that I'm so close to a fire, the egg feels like it's dancing in my pocket. I can't wait any longer, so I clear my throat and ask, "Can I borrow your fire?"

Frank gives me a funny look. "Borrow? What you mean, son? Fire ain't a book you can check out from the library and bring back next week." He chuckles at his own joke, but Frank's smile fades when he sees I'm not laughing.

"I know. I just—I need to put something *in* the fire," I explain.

"What—like trash?" Joe asks.

"We burn trash out here all the time," Frank tells me. "Go ahead—throw it in."

My mouth has never felt so dry. I'm clutching the brown paper bag as hard as I can, but I can't stop my arm from trembling. "Uh . . . you might want to step back."

Joe groans. "It ain't a firecracker, is it?"

Frank frowns and says, "Don't do nothing foolish, Youngblood."

"I won't, sir," I assure him. "But . . . well, I don't know what's going to happen next."

The two men look at each other. Joe shrugs, and Frank says, "Guess there's only one way to find out."

I nod and take a deep breath. Then I toss the crumpled bag into the fire and jump back. For a brief moment, nothing happens. Nothing happens because as soon as the bag touches the flames, everything seems to freeze. The egg doesn't drop into the barrel. Instead, it hovers above the rim, and the flames lick at the brown paper bag until it drifts away as ash. Then the prickly, burnt exterior of the egg softens until it looks like sticky tar. The flames leap a bit higher, and that's when the gold starts to shine through. The tar melts completely, and droplets sizzle as they spatter against the steel drum.

Frank looks as awestruck as I feel. "Boy—what'd you put in there?" he asks.

"It's an egg," I say simply.

"A golden egg!" Joe exclaims.

He steps forward as if to reach for it, but Frank swats his arm away from the flames. "Leave it be, Joe."

The egg is small, and yet its golden surface somehow serves as a mirror, showing each of us our reflection. I peer into the flames and see myself not in a junkyard but on a desolate ridge surrounded by razor-sharp rocks. I gasp, and the men beside me do the same. I can't tell what they're seeing, but they sound as surprised and confused as I am.

Suddenly, there's a loud CRACK! We all jump and watch breathlessly as the golden sphere shatters. Yet even with its surface cracked, the egg holds together long enough for a strong gust of wind to hurl it up into the dark sky. The fire in the drum is extinguished, and the yard instantly becomes cold and dim. All I can see is a trail of orange sparks leading upward. A moment later, the egg explodes with a soft poof. I shiver as gold dust rains down on us.

We all stand there in the darkness, waiting for something remarkable to descend. A full minute goes by, and I start to shift from foot to foot. Then my neck starts to ache from looking up at the sky, but still nothing happens.

Finally, Frank asks, "Is it gone?"

It never occurred to me that the phoenix might fly away! I cross my fingers and keep my eyes glued to the sky. The storm clouds gradually break apart, and the sun pokes through once more. "It can't be. . . ." If it *is* gone, what will I tell Vik?

Joe mutters something about the cold and reaches into his pocket for a book of matches. He strikes one, and in the brief flash of light, I realize something is perched on my shoulder. I almost swat it away, but some instinct stops my hand. There, nestled against the folds of my fleece hood, is the tiniest bird I've ever seen.

It's a bit smaller than a hummingbird, but its feathers are as brightly colored. Its green eyes gleam like emeralds, and it has a golden crest on top of its red head. Long purple tail feathers trail down my arm, and its breast is as blue as the flame from a Bunsen burner. This baby bird must be frightened—or cold—because it trembles as it snuggles against me.

The match expires, and Joe lights another. This time he manages to toss it into the steel drum. The flame struggles to take hold, but smoke slowly rises above the rim.

"Gonna take forever to get this fire going again," Joe mutters.

Something about the smoke brings the little bird to life. It perks up and makes a sound like a cat meowing. I wonder if it's hungry. What do you feed a baby phoenix? The dragons in Ma's care craved anything sweet. Are newborn phoenixes the same way?

Joe lights another match and tosses it into the drum, but this one fizzles out. The tiny bird lifts off my shoulder, flies on unsteady wings, and very nearly misses the rim of the drum. Frustrated, Joe tosses one more lit match inside the drum, but this time the phoenix makes a sneezing sound, and a stream of fire shoots out of its hooked beak. The drum ignites immediately, and the bird perches there for a moment, content to be licked by the flames.

"Now, *that's* a fire!" Joe says, impressed.

"You sure it can stand being so close?" Frank asks me.

I'm not sure of anything, but I have to trust that the baby phoenix knows what it needs, since I don't. Suddenly, my phone rings. I thought my battery was depleted, but when I pull the phone out of my back pocket, I see that it's fully charged. I take the call but don't even have a chance to say hello before Ma's frantic voice booms in my ear.

"Where are you, boy? Don't you know you can't be out in the street after dark? You tell Vonn to bring you home right now!"

"Uh—Vonn had to leave, so . . . I tried to find my own way home, but . . . I got lost."

Ma explodes. I can't tell if she's mad at Vonn or at me, but I have to hold the phone away from my ear for a little while. Frank comes over and takes the phone from my hand.

"Hello? This is Frank Johnson. Your boy's all right, ma'am. He just lost track of time and then got a little turned around. No need for alarm."

I take out my notebook and show Frank the address of the rooming house. He glances at it and assures Ma we'll be there in ten minutes before handing the phone back to me.

"I'll be waiting for you out front," Ma says, a bit calmer than before. "And I'll call your poor mother to let her know you're all right. She's been worried sick. From now on, you keep that fancy phone of yours charged, you hear me?"

"Yes, ma'am," I say respectfully.

"Now hurry up and bring your butt home," she snaps.

Ma ends the call before I can say anything else. Frank must think I need cheering up because he says, "Your gran ain't mad at you, Youngblood. She's just worried, and worry comes out kinda loud sometimes."

I don't correct Frank. Even though he has just witnessed the birth of a phoenix, I don't know if he'd believe me if I told him Ma is the witch I work for and not my grandmother.

"We're not far from where you're staying," Frank

tells me. Then he nods at the purring phoenix and says, "Grab your . . . er, pet. We best be on our way."

Easier said than done! I look at the little bird perched on the rim of the steel drum and know I can't just reach out and pluck it from the fire.

"Try calling it," Joe suggests.

"I don't know its name," I say, mostly to myself. But I step back anyway and call to the bird. "It's time to go home. Come on—time to go." When nothing happens, I pat my shoulder, and the bird reluctantly pulls itself away from the fire and lands on my shoulder once more. I'm not sure if the phoenix will be too hot to touch, so I pull my sleeve down over my hand and reach for it. Its silken feathers are warm, but the baby phoenix is still trembling. Putting it in my bag doesn't seem like a good idea, so I decide on the only other alternative.

"I need to put you in my pocket for a while," I explain. Carefully wrapping the bird's long tail feathers around its small body, I tuck the tiny phoenix in the front pocket of my hoodie. It doesn't seem to mind, maybe because it remembers the dark warmth of its egg. I say goodbye to Joe and let Frank steer me out of the junkyard.

When we reach the street, he takes a deep breath and looks up at the sky. "I've seen a lot of things in my day, but I ain't never seen nothing like that before. Where'd you get that egg, Youngblood?"

"It's not mine," I tell him. "A friend in Brooklyn asked me to look after it for him."

Frank nods and points in the direction we'll be heading. He starts to walk, and I follow.

"Well, you seemed to know just what to do. Guess you were meant to have it."

After a few minutes, we turn onto Martin Luther King Drive. I look up the block and see Ma standing on the stoop with her arms folded across her chest. To my surprise, Frank starts to chuckle.

"That you, Ma?" he hollers as we draw closer. "I mighta known this boy was one of yours."

Ma unfolds her arms and hurries down the stairs to meet us at the gate. "Li'l Frankie Johnson—is that you?" She gives him a warm hug and says, "How long has it been?"

Frank laughs and replies, "I wasn't much older than this boy here when I saw you last, Ma."

"Well, thanks for bringing Jax home. Why don't you come inside for a while. You hungry? Miss E. has laid out quite a spread."

"Don't mind if I do," Frank says with a smile.

When Ma turns to climb back up the front stairs, I tug on Frank's coat. "Uh—Mr. Johnson, do you mind not telling Ma about . . ."

Frank studies me for a couple of seconds before nodding. "Sure thing, Youngblood." Then he winks and adds, "Your secret's safe with me."

Ma's so busy taking Frank's coat and introducing him to Mrs. Benjamin that she doesn't notice when I slip upstairs to deposit the baby phoenix in my room. I make a cozy nest out of a towel and set it on my bed, hoping the bird won't get cold and decide to start another fire. I snap a quick photo and email it to Vik before calling Mama to give her a summary of my first day in Chicago. I tell her all about Vonn and Giordano's but don't mention Frank or the phoenix. For now, I just want to keep the beautiful little bird to myself.

I wish I could eat dinner in my room, but that would just make people suspicious. So I carefully slide the towel under my cot and quietly slip out of my room—only to bump right into Quayesha.

She gives me a funny look, but then she smiles and asks, "You have a good time with Vonn today?"

I nod, eager to tell the truth whenever I can. "You were right—he knows everything about Chicago."

"Vonn's a walking encyclopedia." Quayesha folds her arms across her chest and adds, "Strange that he left you on your own, though."

I shrug and say, "He must have had something important to do. It's okay. Vonn gave me directions. The city's basically a grid—just like Manhattan. I kept the lake on my right side and headed north. I wasn't really lost. I just . . . took a detour."

Quayesha narrows her eyes. "A 'detour,' huh? Why'd you do that?"

"Why?" I swallow hard and think fast. "Uh . . . I thought I saw a shortcut, but I was wrong. It was a dead end."

Quayesha nods, but I can tell she's not buying it. "It's a good thing Frank found you. Ma was really worried about you, Jax."

"If Ma was really worried about me, she would have kept an eye on me herself instead of unloading me on a total stranger." That's what I *want* to say, but instead, I fake a grin and agree with Quayesha. "Yeah, I guess I got lucky. Excuse me—nature calls."

I squeeze past Quayesha and head straight for the bathroom. I close the door and wait until I hear her going down the creaky wooden staircase. Then I pull out my phone and try calling Vik.

"Pick up, pick up," I whisper to my reflection in the mirror above the sink.

When I hear Mrs. Patel's voice on the line, I make sure to ask for Vik in a polite, patient way, even though I'm desperate to talk to my friend. His mom asks me about Chicago, and I try to answer her questions as briefly as possible without seeming rude. Finally, she sets down the phone and calls her son. I hear the soft rumble of Vik's feet running down the stairs before he picks up the phone. He must not be alone, because he's whispering, but I can still tell how excited Vik is.

"Jax! I can't believe the egg hatched already. The baby phoenix looks so cute. What are you going to call it?"

"I don't know. It's so tiny! And sleepy. I'm just trying to keep it warm. Do you know what to feed a baby phoenix?"

"The old phoenix used to eat gumballs, so give those a try," Vik tells me.

"Gumballs?" I ask, surprised by his suggestion.

"We used to toss them up in the air, and the phoenix would swoop down from its tree and gobble them up!" Vik recalls with a laugh.

"I'll have to get some from the store tomorrow. How's Brooklyn?"

Vik sighs. "Kind of hectic, actually. So many adults have fallen under the sleeping spell! The mayor is recommending that people stay indoors until they figure out the cause. Ma was right—it seems to affect grown-ups more than kids."

"And how's your sister?" I ask.

"She's not getting any better," Vik says. Then he lowers his voice even more and adds, "Kavi set off the smoke alarm yesterday. I took the blame, but Mummy knows something's going on. I've spent my entire allowance on sweets to keep my little sister happy, but she's never satisfied! Can you ask Ma what I should do?"

I think for a moment before I respond. I have to tell Vik the truth, so I admit, "Actually, I haven't told Ma about the phoenix yet."

"Why not?" Vik asks. "She's, like, an expert on magical creatures, right?"

"I know, but . . . she's been so busy with the convention and . . . well . . . what if she decides to send the phoenix back to Sis?"

"What if that's the best place for the phoenix to be, Jax? I wish Ma would send my little sister away!"

"Very funny, Vik. I'm serious. What if Sis taking the dragon away is what made Kavi start to change? If Ma sends the phoenix away, I might change, too."

"Hmm. I didn't think of that," Vik says. "I definitely can't handle my little sister *and* my best friend breathing fire all the time."

I laugh before asking, "How's Kenny?"

Vik sighs. "Are you sitting down?"

I perch on the edge of the claw-foot tub and wait for Vik to go on.

He takes a deep breath and says, "Kenny thinks he'll be able to *fly* soon. He hasn't grown wings yet, but . . . his feet are tingling, and he can already levitate a little. I wish you were here to help us make sense of everything."

I think for a moment. How can I help my friends when I'm so far away? "Listen—I met this really cool guy, Vonn. He knows just about everything about Chicago, and I think he knows a lot about magic, too. When I see him tomorrow, I'll tell him what's going on. Maybe he'll know what we should do."

"Or you could just tell Ma," Vik counters.

"Ma's different these days," I tell him.

"Different how?"

I sigh. "I don't know. I get the feeling she doesn't trust me."

"Well, you *are* keeping a pretty big secret from her right now!" Vik reminds me.

"True. There's another, younger witch in Ma's coven. Maybe I can ask her for advice."

"Please ask *somebody*—and do it soon!" Vik pleads. "I don't know how much longer I can hide Kavi's condition from my parents."

I promise Vik I'll call him again tomorrow. Then I hang up, slip my phone back in my pocket, and head downstairs to join the others for dinner. I don't pay much attention to the conversation taking place around me, but my ears perk up when I hear Ma ask Frank for a favor.

"You know the South Side better than most, Frank.

Could you see if any factories have been acting funny lately?"

"Nothing funny about pollution," Frank says. "We got more than our fair share of smokestacks on the South Side, but I'll ask around for you, Ma."

"I'd appreciate that, Frank. I already know who the culprit is, but I need proof."

Frank nods and turns to compliment Miss Ellabelle on her food as she serves him a second helping of meat loaf. Miss E. is a lot more polite to Frank than she is to me, maybe because he isn't an overnight guest.

When I'm finally able to get back to my room, I search all the pockets on my knapsack until I come up with a lone piece of gum. I can tell that it has been in my bag for a while because the foil wrapper is long gone. But when I place the stick of gum near the phoenix, it sniffs it excitedly before snapping off tiny bits with its golden beak.

When it has eaten about a third of the stick of gum, the phoenix curls up in its makeshift nest and goes back to sleep. I could stare at this feathery gem forever, but it's time for me to turn in, too. I dash to the bathroom to brush my teeth, then put on my pajamas and crawl into bed. With the phoenix softly snoring beside me, I fall asleep right away. That night in my dreams I hear the man in the mirror say, "The wait is almost over, my son."

8

When I wake up the next morning, I know right away that the phoenix isn't sleeping in its towel nest. I know because as soon as I open my eyes, I see red. The phoenix is nestled on my pillow, its little body so close to my face that I feel its feathers tickling my nose as I breathe. I can even smell the faint trace of mint on its breath from the gum it had for dinner last night.

I know that I ought to tell Ma about the phoenix. But as I watch the tiny flame-colored bird sleep, I feel compelled to keep it to myself a little while longer. The dragons never belonged to me, so I didn't feel all that attached to them. Kavita was the first person they saw, and maybe she felt then the same way I feel now. Protective. Possessive.

Even though I begged Ma for weeks to take me to the convention, I no longer have any real interest in going.

All I want to do is spend time with my new feathery friend. It needs me—Ma doesn't.

I hear the witches heading downstairs for breakfast, but when Ma knocks on my door, I quickly cover the phoenix, moan loudly, and tell her I have a stomachache. Ma pokes her head inside my room and studies me for a few seconds.

"I'll bring you some dry toast," she says finally.

"No!" I reply hastily. "I mean, I think maybe I better skip breakfast today and just stay in bed for a little longer."

Ma watches me for several uncomfortable seconds before saying, "Suit yourself. I'll tell Vonn to come by around noon again. If you're feeling up for it, you can go out with him, but this time, he's to bring you straight back here by five o'clock. Understand?"

"Yes, ma'am. Have fun at the convention."

Ma grunts and pulls her head out of the room so she can close the door. I sigh with relief and lift the covers to admire the sleeping phoenix. We stay in bed for at least another hour—until I'm sure the witches have left for the convention. Then I get up and get dressed, carefully folding the phoenix into the front pocket of my hoodie once more. When I hear Miss Ellabelle's vacuum, I hurry downstairs and try to sneak out unnoticed. But just as my hand grasps the knob of the front door, the vacuum stops and Miss Ellabelle hollers at me.

"Wait just a minute, young man. Where do you think you're going?"

"Uh . . . I'm meeting Vonn," I mumble, keeping my eyes on the floor. "He's going to show me more of the city."

She frowns and folds her arms across her chest. "Ma said you were to put something in your belly and wait for that young thug to pick you up at noon." She points at the grandfather clock in the parlor. It's not yet eleven o'clock.

I know it's not a good idea to pick a fight right now, but I don't like that word. "Vonn's not a thug," I tell her. "He's a . . ." There's no point telling Miss Ellabelle that Vonn's a Watcher, so I finish my sentence with something just as true: "Vonn's my friend. And I know it's early. I'm just running out to get something from the store," I tell her, which is also true.

"What sort of *thing*?" she asks. Before I can think of a convincing lie for why I suddenly need gumballs, Miss Ellabelle rushes toward the door and grabs me by the arm. She hauls me into the dining room and orders me to sit down. "I won't have it said that a guest of mine left this house without a proper meal."

"That's okay, Miss Ellabelle," I assure her. "I'll eat later on." I put my hand on my belly and groan a little for effect. "My stomach doesn't feel so good."

"And I suppose you think my meat loaf is to blame!" she says huffily.

"No!" I insist. "It's probably all the excitement. Plus, the UR was really jerky . . . and I had pizza yesterday. I'm lactose intolerant."

"Then I've got just the thing," she says with an unnerving grin.

Miss Ellabelle heads to the kitchen, and I consider making a dash for the door. But she might chase after me—or tell Ma that I snuck out on my own. So I stay put and await my punishment. That's really the only way to describe what's in the bowl she places in front of me a moment later.

"What is it?" I ask, dipping my spoon into the odorless gray slop.

"Gruel. Best thing for your sour stomach. Go on, eat up!"

I glance around the room for a potted plant or an open window where I could discreetly dump the steaming gruel, but Miss Ellabelle stands right next to me instead of returning to her vacuuming. After a while she starts tapping her toe on the hardwood floor, and

I realize she won't leave my side until every last drop of slop is consumed.

My stomach didn't really hurt before this unexpected and unappetizing breakfast, but it *definitely* feels funky by the time I finish choking down Miss Ellabelle's porridge. I burp and quickly say, "Excuse me," but the chef takes my indigestion as a compliment.

"See? Gruel is guaranteed to bring up all the gas that's got your belly in a knot."

Somehow I manage to thank her as she clears away my bowl and spoon and heads back to the kitchen. I creep out to the foyer just as Vonn jogs up the front steps.

"Bye!" I yell before dashing out the door.

"Sup, Brooklyn?" Vonn asks, pulling me into a half hug as we shake hands. "You feeling any better?"

"Much worse, actually," I tell him as we head for the street. "Miss Ellabelle made me eat a gallon of gruel."

Vonn tips his head back and laughs. His gem-covered teeth flash in the sunlight. Today he is wearing all black—sneakers, jeans, hoodie, and shades. Diamond studs gleam in each earlobe, and on his neck is a tattoo I didn't notice before: a single black feather.

"Ma wasn't too happy that I left you on your own yesterday, but I knew you'd find your way back."

I nod and decide not to tell Vonn how anxious I felt when he disappeared after showing me the Garden of the Phoenix. Instead, I take a deep breath and ask him what I really want to know: "Can you read minds?"

Vonn shakes his head and says, "Mind reading takes a different set of skills. Me, I just observe."

"So . . . you probably noticed that I was acting kind of funny yesterday."

Vonn shrugs. "We just met, so it's hard for me to know what you're like when everything's cool. However, I couldn't help but notice that you were carrying some precious cargo."

"I *knew* you knew!" I cry. "But how—was it really that obvious? I did try to keep the egg hidden."

"It takes real expertise to hide something that powerful."

Vonn's serious, but I can't help laughing. "Powerful? It's the tiniest bird I've ever seen." I pull the phoenix from my pocket and hold it out for Vonn to see.

He doesn't remove his dark sunglasses, but behind the black lenses, I see Vonn's pupils light up as he examines the beautiful baby bird. He whistles and says, "Haven't seen one of those in a very, very long time."

The baby phoenix yawns and seems to enjoy seeing its reflection in Vonn's shades. Then it spots a vibrant tree, and the bird lifts itself off my palm to fly into its branches. The young maple tree is little more than a sapling, but its skinny trunk is crowned by leaves that have already turned an autumnal shade of neon orange. The phoenix must be confused, because it hops from branch to branch as if expecting to be warmed by flames.

I walk over and hold up my hand. "It's probably warmer in my pocket," I say. The tiny phoenix seems disappointed, and before long it hops onto my finger and lets me tuck it into my pocket once more.

"What are you going to do with it?" Vonn asks. When I don't respond, he adds, "I assume you have some sort of plan."

Plan? Other than keeping the phoenix a secret from Ma, I don't have a plan at all. "If you had a baby phoenix, what would *you* do?" I ask.

"Well, I guess I'd try to figure out why it came to me."

"That's easy," I tell Vonn. "It came to me because my friend Vik asked me to take care of it for him."

"So it wasn't always in your possession?"

I shake my head. "I'd only had it for one day before it hatched. Vik kept it in his sock drawer since last summer."

"Then you were chosen," Vonn says somberly.

I think about that for a moment. Is it possible the

phoenix waited to be born until it was with me? Then the most delicious smell wafts down the block, and I lose my ability to concentrate. A short, elderly woman is up ahead with a red cooler. Her long black hair is streaked with silver and trails down her back in a single braid. The woman wheels the cooler along the sidewalk, and inside are tamales. I know because a girl around my age is a few paces ahead of the woman calling out to passersby: "Hot tamales! Best in Bronzeville!"

"Hungry?" Vonn asks.

"Actually, I need to get some gum to feed the phoenix," I tell him.

He points to a store on the corner and waits outside while I go in to stock up on different gum shapes and flavors. When I come back out, I hear the girl across the street pleading with someone.

"Don't—please! You have to pay! You *have to*!"

Three teenage boys are walking away from the food vendors with tamales in their hands. Two of them have already started peeling the banana leaves to devour the tasty filling inside. The girl sounds like she's about to cry, and the old woman—her grandmother, I think— simply holds out her hand, wordlessly and rightfully expecting payment for her food.

"Thanks for lunch!" one blond boy calls over his shoulder before crossing the street.

His friends follow, and the one with skin as brown as mine sneers, "What are you gonna do—call the cops?"

When the girl dares to pursue them, the third boy, who is wearing a red baseball cap, reaches out a hand to give the girl a shove. She loses her balance and falls to the ground, which only makes the bullies laugh louder. I watch the scene unfold and feel a fire burning in my belly.

Before long they're on our side of the street and nearly bump into me and Vonn as we stand outside the convenience store.

"I hate bullies," I say to no one in particular.

Vonn leans down and whispers in my ear, "What you gonna do about it, Brooklyn?"

"What *can* I do?"

Vonn puts his hand on my shoulder and turns me away from the girl and her grandmother. He gently taps his finger against my chest and says, "Start with your intention, Jax, not your limitations. Think about what you want."

I watch as the girl picks herself up off the ground and brushes the dirt off her clothes. I didn't notice before that her left foot turns inward. She was quick to chase after the thieves, but now she moves slowly as she goes back over to her grandmother. If the girl is hurt, she's hiding her pain. I know how that feels. She can't protect herself from bullies, but she can protect her grandmother from knowing how much they hurt her.

I want to make them pay. I don't say it out loud, but I know that Vonn is watching me. The bullies come out of the store holding beverages to go with their stolen tamales. I glare at them and wish I were bigger and

stronger—someone they'd fear instead of just a scrawny kid they can push aside.

The phoenix is nestled in my pocket, and my hands are hanging at my side, but I feel fire warming the tips of my fingers. I curl my hands into fists, and that seems to concentrate the power I feel growing inside me. I stand there like that—my fists pressed against my legs—my eyes trained on the three boys until their laughter starts to sputter.

The tallest boy, the one in the red cap, clears his throat and then starts to cough. One of the others pats him on the back, but it doesn't help.

"Ho . . . hot . . . HOT!" he gasps as his face turns pink.

He cries for water, and so his blond friend offers him his can of soda, but then the can explodes, spraying them all with brown cola. They start blaming each other as the choking boy races back into the store, desperate for a drink to calm the fire burning in his throat.

I watch them with a small smile on my face. I don't want to hurt them, but right now they look ridiculous. "I guess those tamales were too hot to handle," I say with a smirk.

"You did that," Vonn says flatly. "You humiliated them."

My smile broadens into a grin. "Yeah—I did!" I finally look up at Vonn and see that he isn't smiling.

Vonn gives my shoulder a slight push, and we start walking again. "So . . . how's it feel, Brooklyn?"

"What do you mean?" I ask, somewhat annoyed by Vonn's question. If he would just smile, maybe I wouldn't have this strange feeling in my belly (it's not indigestion).

"You made them pay for what they did to that girl."

"Yeah. I guess I did."

"How do you think it makes her feel?" Vonn asks.

I shrug. "I don't know," I say testily.

"Guess there's no way for you *to* know, since you never asked her what *she* wanted." Vonn pauses a moment and then adds, "Right?"

I can tell Vonn's disappointed in me, and somehow that makes me angry. If I was supposed to do something else, why didn't he tell me? "I guess I messed up," I say sullenly. "That's the only thing I'm really good at."

"You're good at a lot of things," Vonn says, "but using magic is new, and it'll take a while for you to get the hang of it."

I nod, humbled but also grateful that Vonn's taking the time to explain all this to me.

"Tell me about your intention," he says. "Remember when I asked what you wanted?"

I nod again, and Vonn continues.

"Did you want to help that girl or to make those boys pay for what they did to her?"

"Both?" I'm not sure what to say, because I'm not entirely sure what I was trying to achieve.

Vonn's next question catches me off guard. "Who's your favorite superhero?"

"Miles Morales," I answer without hesitation.

"A'ight. Now think about the classic comic-book

superhero. When Miles wants to save somebody, he just swoops in with his cape flying behind him and does what he thinks is right."

I smile as I remember how long it took for Miles to learn how to act and dress like Spider-Man—*his* version of Spider-Man. I wonder if a Watcher like Vonn ever goes to the movies.

"Saving people is cool," he says, "and so is leaping over tall buildings."

That's Superman, actually. He has a cape and Spider-Man doesn't, but I don't bother to correct Vonn. Instead, I focus on learning the lesson he's trying to teach me.

"But if you want to *serve* someone, then you need to act like a waiter in a restaurant. You can't just show up at someone's table and give them what you want them to eat. You're a waiter—you're there to take their order. That's how you make sure they get what *they* want."

Vonn pauses to give me a minute to think about what he's said. I stop walking and look over at the girl and her grandmother. "Can we cross the street?" I ask Vonn.

"It's your move, Brooklyn. I'll follow your lead."

I check for traffic and then head to the other side of the street. As I near the food vendors, the girl lifts her head and says, "Do you want a tamal? Best in Bronzeville."

Her voice has lost some of its confidence, but she

smiles when I nod and reach into my bag for my wallet. I order four tamales, even though I've still got a belly full of gruel.

"Want a bag?" the girl asks.

I nod, and she puts them in a brown paper bag for me. "Anything else?"

I glance back at Vonn, clear my throat, and say, "I'd like to pay for the tamales those boys stole."

For a moment, none of us says a word. I'm blushing, and so is the girl. I'm not sure her grandmother understands, because the girl turns to her and says something in a language I've never heard before.

"Please," I say, holding out Mama's crisp twenty-dollar bill. She said to save it for emergencies, but I think this is just as important.

The girl opens a zippered pouch tied around her grandmother's waist and counts out my change. She hands it to me and says, "Maltyox. Thank you."

I put the money back in my wallet and wonder if I have done enough. "What language is that? It doesn't sound like Spanish—I'm learning that in school."

The girl smiles and proudly says, "It's K'iche', pero yo también hablo español. I'm Itzel."

"Mi nombre es Jaxon," I tell her, hoping my Spanish is correct.

Suddenly, her grandmother sways, and Vonn steps forward to steady her.

"Grandmother!"

"Let's find your grandmother somewhere to sit down," Vonn suggests. He guides the weary woman over to a nearby bus shelter. Itzel holds her grandmother's hand. I grab the cooler and wheel it over. Another man there is already fast asleep and snoring so loudly he can't hear the bus pulling up to the curb. I look at his clothes and see the telltale white flakes on his jacket. There are some on Itzel's grandmother's clothing as well.

"Is there a park around here?" I ask.

Itzel nods, though she looks confused. "Washington Park is just a few blocks that way."

"Do you live far from here?"

When Itzel shakes her head, I turn to Vonn and ask, "Could you help them get back home?"

"Sure. What's your plan, Brooklyn?"

"I'm going to see if I can find some silver root growing in the park," I tell him. Then I remember what Vonn said earlier about being a waiter. I turn to Itzel and explain my idea. "My boss showed me how to find a plant that will help your grandmother stay awake. Would it be okay if I brought you some?"

Itzel nods eagerly and points to a nearby apartment building. "That's where we live."

"I'll be back as soon as I can," I assure her. Then I hurry up the block and scour the park for the familiar purple triangular leaves. It takes a while, but after twenty minutes of searching, I find a couple of plants growing near a big oak tree. I pull them out of the ground gently and shake the dirt loose just like Ma taught me to do. Then I race back to Itzel's building. She's watching for me at the window and buzzes me in.

When I reach their studio apartment, Vonn is nowhere to be seen, but Itzel has made her grandmother comfortable in bed. The phoenix stirs in my pocket, so I pull it out. Itzel smiles and tells her grandmother to look at the beautiful little bird. She responds in K'iche', so Itzel translates for me.

"My grandmother says it looks like a quetzal, the national bird of Guatemala."

Itzel's grandmother holds out her hand, and the little bird flies over to her. I wonder if I should tell them it's a phoenix, but instead, I leave the bird snuggled against the old woman's neck and join Itzel in the kitchen.

"What are you doing?" I ask.

"Making my grandmother some chocolate. I can

grind up the root and mix it in. That's how I always take my medicine. My grandmother told me that in Guatemala, long before the conquistadores invaded our land, the people turned to the hechicera when they were ill."

"What's a hechicera?"

"A sorceress who could heal the sick or use magic to solve people's problems. The hechicera often used chocolate for her potions, since most people in our country drink it every day. Want some?"

I nod eagerly and watch as Itzel breaks apart a bar of thin, dark chocolate. She places the squares in a saucepan and adds water. Then she carefully turns on the stove and stirs the mixture with a whisk until the chocolate has dissolved. She pours in some milk and then reaches for a bottle of cinnamon.

"I've never had hot chocolate with cinnamon," I tell her, "but it sure smells good."

"Sometimes we add a chili pepper, too," she explains.

Itzel keeps stirring until there's foam on the thick brown liquid. Then she turns off the burner and carefully pours the chocolate into three mugs. She hands one to me and then starts grinding the silver root with a mortar and pestle for her grandmother.

Before I can take my first sip, the phoenix flutters over to the rim of my mug and dips its beak into the hot chocolate!

"Hey!" I cry.

Itzel and her grandmother both laugh. After a few more sips, the phoenix abandons me and flies back over to the elderly woman now that she, too, has a mug of hot chocolate in her hands. The little bird takes two sips and then watches approvingly as Itzel's grandmother drinks the rest herself. I wonder if the silver root will also make the phoenix more alert. It sleeps a lot when it's with me, but right now the bird is listening intently as Itzel's grandmother softly sings it a song. I can't understand the words, but I think maybe the phoenix can.

"Thank you for helping us, Jax," Itzel says with a shy smile. "Sometimes I feel like we're invisible. Things happen, and people just walk on by or look the other way. But you didn't."

"Well, I wasn't sure what to do at first," I admit, "but Vonn taught me how to be a good waiter."

Itzel looks confused. Then she cries, "Oh—I almost forgot! Your friend said to meet him at the Fountain of Time."

"The Fountain of Time?"

Itzel explains that it's a sculpture at the far end of Washington Park. "It's where the Midway begins," she says.

I already know how to get there, so I thank Itzel again for the delicious hot chocolate, wave to her grandmother, and pocket the phoenix as I head off to find Vonn.

9

"You found me," Vonn says with a grin. "You'll know the neighborhood better than I do by the time you leave."

I step into the fountain and sit next to him on the ledge. It's more of a shallow pool than a fountain, really. The water has been drained, so our feet rest on the dry concrete.

"Are you hungry?" I ask, pulling the paper bag of tamales out of my knapsack. Vonn accepts two, and we don't say much while we eat. Itzel didn't put any chili peppers in my hot chocolate, but her grandmother definitely put some in her salsa! Vonn doesn't seem fazed by the heat, but my eyes start to water, and I need more than a few sips of water from the bottle I carry in my bag. I have to wonder if I really did make that bully choke on his tamal. Maybe I just wanted to believe I had the power to punish those boys. Maybe Ma was right only to teach me about foraging for healing plants.

I look across the empty pool at a long line of stone figures. They are crouching at the start of the line, and standing tall in the middle, but by the end, they're crouching or crawling once more. This seems like a strange place to meet. Next to us, staring at the line of people in the distance, is a tall, hooded figure who looks kind of sinister. He's holding some sort of staff under his stone cloak, but it doesn't have a blade at the top.

"That's not the Grim Reaper, is it?" I ask, nodding up at the statue.

"Father Time," Vonn replies. "And those folks," he says, pointing to the stone marchers, "are supposed to represent humanity. There's a hundred of them altogether."

I take another bite of my tamal and search the wall of people for a face like mine. There are old folks and little kids, couples embracing, soldiers marching, and one man on horseback. Not one of the figures looks like somebody in my family.

"Why'd you want to meet here? Is there something special about this place?"

Vonn picks up the paper bag and puts his banana leaves inside. He holds it out to me, and I do the same with mine. "This sculpture was inspired by a poem, 'The Paradox of Time.' Ever heard of it?"

I shake my head and wonder what all the stone people across the pool have to do with time.

"People like to say 'time flies,' but this poet says it's the other way around: 'Time stays, we go!'"

"You don't. If you were here when DuSable was around, then you're pretty old, Vonn, even if you don't look your age."

Vonn smiles, but his diamond-encrusted teeth don't sparkle like before. If he took his sunglasses off right now, I suspect the light in his eyes would be dim.

"As a Watcher, I've lived more lifetimes than I can count. I've watched the world change around me without ever being able to change it myself." Vonn pauses to heave a sorrowful sigh. "It wears on a body, seeing so much but doing so little."

I'm not sure what to say. I've never really thought about immortality, but in most of the stories I've read, the person who thinks they want to live forever winds up changing their mind in the end. Like Sis said last spring—death is part of what makes us human. Would we value our lives if we knew they'd go on forever?

"I want you to know something, Jaxon. No matter

what happens, I want you to know that meeting you has given me hope. I'd almost forgotten what that feels like. . . ."

Vonn gets up, but when I try to do the same, he puts his hand on my shoulder and gently pushes me back down.

"Are you leaving me again?" I ask. I know how to get back to the rooming house, but Ma won't be happy if I show up alone.

"There's someone I want you to meet. Actually, it's someone you already know—someone from Brooklyn." I'm not sure if I look anxious or confused, but Vonn gives my shoulder a reassuring squeeze as he steps out of the dry reflecting pool. "I hope you'll give him a chance, Jax. I hope you'll hear what he has to say. It's important."

"Will I see you tomorrow?"

Vonn shrugs. "That depends."

"On what?"

"On what you decide after you talk to my friend."

I have other questions I want to ask, but Vonn just pulls up his hood and walks away. The wind picks up, and I shiver as dead leaves scrape across the empty pool to form a bank against the distant wall. *Time stays, we go!* I glance up at Father Time and then check the actual time on my phone. Ma said to be home by five p.m. I've got less than an hour.

Five minutes go by, then five more. Finally, I sense someone standing behind me. My hand instinctively slips inside my pocket and curls around the sleeping phoenix.

"Remember me, kid? I remember you."

I know that voice. Even without turning around, I know that Ma was right—Blue is in Chicago. But Vonn said I would be meeting his "friend." He couldn't have meant Blue—could he?

"Mind if I sit down? It's been a long day."

Blue groans as he takes Vonn's place beside me on the ledge. I don't want to, but I turn to look at him and see that he hasn't changed much since the last time we met. Even without his signature tattoos, Blue looks as devious as ever. I remember those cold gray eyes and the silver loop resting just above lips that seem permanently twisted into a sneer.

"What do you want?" I ask in a voice as cold as the wind.

Blue pretends to be offended. "Is that any way to greet an old friend from back home?"

I glare at him and say, "We're not friends."

"We could be."

I look around, hoping to find Vonn watching us from a distance, but he seems to have vanished.

Blue pulls a white paper bag from his coat pocket. Even before the sugary scent wafts my way, I know he's brought doughnuts. He holds the bag out, but I shake my head.

"You sure? They're paczki."

"Pouch key?"

Blue laughs. "Close. Paczki are Polish doughnuts." He sinks his teeth into one and, with his mouth full, says, "Heavenly!"

Powdered sugar flies out of his open mouth, and red filling spills out of the doughnut onto his white T-shirt. I shift farther away from Blue and say, "I don't have all day, so just say what you came to say."

Blue wipes his mouth with the back of his hand and chews quickly so he can speak more clearly. "Right— I want to respect your curfew. Ma keeps you on a tight leash, huh?" I just scowl at Blue, so he hurries on. "Let me start by saying how much I appreciate this opportunity to share my point of view."

"I'm only here because Vonn asked me to give you a chance."

Blue nods and says, "Vonn's a good guy—and a true ally. Which is what we all need in these trying times. . . ."

I sigh loudly and check the time on my phone. Blue takes the hint and finally gets to the point.

"When I saw you last, I told you I'd be back. I told you

I wasn't the only one willing to stand up to Sis. There's going to be a trial, you know. The Supreme Council has agreed to hear my complaint."

Blue did say something like that the last time I saw him at the emporium. But Trub said not to take him seriously. "What's that got to do with me?"

"Do you know what a subpoena is, kid?"

"Sure. My mom's a paralegal."

"Is she, now? No wonder she took that terrible landlord of yours to court. There's going to be a trial here in Chicago at the witch convention. You should have been served with a subpoena weeks ago, but my sources tell me you haven't responded. I'm here now because I want to make sure I'm going to see you in court tomorrow."

I need a moment to take in everything Blue has just told me. Why didn't Ma mention a trial, and why didn't I receive the subpoena? "Are you suing Sis?"

"Not quite. But she has to be held accountable for that stunt she pulled back in Brooklyn. She's holding those creatures—my friends—hostage in Palmara. It's not right."

It almost feels as if Blue is speaking another language. "Palmara?"

Blue blinks with surprise. Then he frowns and shakes his head like he's disappointed. Yet his voice is surprisingly kind when he explains, "Palmara's the realm of magic, kid. What's Ma been teaching you?"

"Not much," I mutter, and then immediately feel guilty for talking bad about Ma. She taught me how to find silver root, and that helped Itzel's grandmother. If Ma has kept other things from me, she must have a good reason.

"Why don't you have a doughnut, and I'll tell you everything you need to know."

I figure it's safe to sit with Blue just for a little while, though I resist the urge to scarf down a jelly doughnut.

"Ask me anything," he says with a straight face. "Unlike some people, I've got nothing to hide."

I ignore his dig at Ma and ask, "Why do you think Sis is holding your 'friends' hostage? Isn't it her job to protect all the magical creatures?"

Blue scoffs. "Protect them from what—freedom? A hostage is someone who's being held against their will. Think back to that night in Brooklyn, Jax. Did those creatures look like they *wanted* to leave with Sis?"

I think of the way Sis peeled the living tattoos off Blue's body. I recall their cries of protest and shake my head. Vik's aunt was the only one who seemed ready to go. "But if they're hostages, that means Sis is only holding them until she gets what she wants—like a ransom."

"Exactly. You're a smart kid, Jax. I can see why Ma wanted you on her team."

Blue's compliment makes me blush, but this time I manage to bite my tongue instead of saying what it's like to be the only member of Ma's team who gets benched all the time.

Blue leans forward and rests his elbows on his knees. "Sis wants to change our world. It's happening already."

He pauses to dramatically sweep his hand across the drained pool, with its piles of dead leaves. I look across the meadow at the flame-colored leaves on the trees and the pedestrians bundled up to keep warm, though it's the middle of summer.

"All these changes are caused by one person who thinks she can keep all the magic to herself." He pauses for effect and then asks, "Did you know Sis has a brother?" The surprise on my faces says it all. "Surely Ma told you about Ranadahy. He and Sis are twins. They used to rule Palmara together."

"What happened?" I ask, somewhat ashamed of my own curiosity.

"Her brother dared to disagree with her, so Sis locked him up in a tower and threw away the key! That was a thousand years ago, and Sis hasn't changed a bit. She's just as stubborn and selfish as she was back then. You know why? Because no one's ever stood up to her—except Ranadahy. He's a powerful wizard, and he's our only hope."

"I thought you said he was locked up."

Blue nods but avoids looking me in the eye. "He is—he was. It's complicated, but I managed to get a message to him."

"What did you say?"

"That Sis no longer has the support of the union. Ma's never told you about that, either, huh? I'm not surprised. The witches had their own federation and still hold their own convention each year. But over time they aligned themselves with other practitioners like me. I was a gatekeeper before—"

"Sis fired you," I say, remembering what L. Roy told me about Blue.

Blue frowns and says, "Technically, I was demoted, but she would gladly have fired me if she thought she could get away with it. That's why people join unions, Jax—to make sure that bosses respect workers' rights. I wanted Ranadahy to know that most of us have lost faith in his sister's ability to serve as Guardian of Palmara."

I think about that for a moment. I haven't met anyone besides Blue who feels that way about Sis, though L. Roy probably made her mad by sending the three baby dragons to Brooklyn. Ma's definitely loyal to Sis, and Vonn never mentioned having a problem with her. Yet he called Blue his friend.

I'm starting to feel confused, which makes me kind of angry. "Why should I believe a word you say?" I demand. "If Ma were here—"

"Ah, your good friend Ma. How's she liking the convention?"

I open my mouth to answer but realize I don't know what to say, since Ma hasn't told me anything about the convention.

"Cat got your tongue? Or maybe you can't say because you don't know much about the secret meetings Ma's been attending. She made sure of that, right? She brought you all the way to Chicago and then kept you out of sight. Almost makes you wonder why Ma bothered to bring you at all."

I get up and grab my knapsack. "I'm not listening to you. You may have fooled Vonn, but Nate said you couldn't be trusted."

"And Ma can? You trust *her*, even though she's done everything in her power to keep us apart. And all *I'm* trying to do is restore balance to our world."

When I turn to go, Blue becomes desperate. "How are your friends?" he calls after me. "Sweet little Kavita and her devoted big brother. And the other one—what's his name again?"

I'm not sure why, but hearing my friends' names makes me turn back to face Blue. "Kenny."

"Right—he's the one who took a fancy to that fairy Sis sent to spy on you. How's Kenny doing these days?"

I say nothing, not wanting to admit to Blue that my friends are having problems. But when Blue pats the fountain's ledge, inviting me to rejoin the conversation, I sit down—as far away from him as possible.

"Things haven't been right since Sis took the last dragon back to Palmara," I admit.

Blue nods and takes a moment to gaze at the wall of humanity on the other side of the fountain. "She closed all the gates that linked the two realms. Sis is a powerful ruler, but she acts out of fear. That's why she banished her brother—she was afraid he would forge an alliance with humans that would bind our worlds together forever. But fear is never as strong as hope. That's what I've got, Jaxon. Hope. I know our world can be so much more than it is right now."

I've never heard Blue talk this way. He sounds earnest. Passionate. "What's in it for you?" I ask skeptically.

Blue laughs and slides the paper bag a little closer to me. I peer inside and finally pluck a fat, powdery doughnut from the bag. Blue waits for me to take a bite before he answers my question.

"Sis calls herself a guardian, but she acts more like a dictator. I just want my friends to be free."

"So you can harvest their powers and sell more potions to gullible people?"

"No. Spells and potions have their place, but they are simply a means to an end. I cast a sedation spell over Brooklyn, but not to hurt anyone—I wanted to help you and your friends."

I don't want to believe Blue, but he sounds sincere. "How does putting everyone to sleep help us?"

"The spell's harmless, really, and it only affects adults. Once they're out of the way, the next generation will be able to make their own choices instead of being told what to do."

The idea of a world without grown-ups excites me but frightens me, too. "But we're just kids," I remind him. "We can't take care of ourselves. We *need* adults."

Blue simply shrugs. "They won't sleep forever. You broke Ma's sleeping spell, remember? I'm just trying to buy you some time."

"Time for what?"

"To think for yourself without some bossy grown-up telling you what to believe—and that includes me."

I must look doubtful, because Blue tries another approach.

"You've heard about the forest fires out in California, right?"

I nod, and he goes on. "Folks were worried about the redwood trees. Some of them are ancient—hundreds, even thousands of years old. And they did burn as the fires swept through. But most of them are still standing. Now the ground around them is ready for new growth—saplings can spring up, and some of them will one day reach the sky. That's the way the world works, Jax. Sometimes you just have to clear a path so the next generation has room to grow."

I feel a bit queasy because everything Blue's saying—even the way he's saying it—sounds perfectly reasonable. But I know I can't trust him. "Our elders are important," I insist. "They share their experiences and their wisdom with us."

"That's true. Little kids would make a lot of bad choices if they didn't have an adult keeping an eye on what they eat and where they go and how they play. But you're not a baby. You wouldn't need to be under surveillance all the time if you shared some of my friends' special abilities."

I think for a moment. It's clear that Blue is dying to

tell me what he's done, but I make him wait a bit longer while I try to piece the puzzle together myself. When he says "friends," he's talking about all the magical creatures that Sis peeled off his body and sent back to Palmara. And "special abilities" means all the things those creatures can do that we humans can't. Like how fairies can fly, and dragons can breathe fire . . .

"That night in the emporium—you did something to us, didn't you?" I ask.

Blue gives me a sideways nod, looking more proud than guilty. "I just let you kids follow your own instincts. You were curious, you wandered around my lab, and . . . you inhaled an experimental gas I've been working on."

With his head still tilted to one side, Blue looks at me, waiting for me to ask him all the questions that are swirling in my mind. But I don't want to give him the satisfaction, so I say nothing. We sit there for several uncomfortable seconds until Blue finally explodes.

"Aw, come on, kid! You must be dying to know what's happening to you and your friends. You're starting to experience symptoms, right?"

"I thought you wanted us kids to make up our own minds. I don't need you to explain what you've done. Kavita is turning into a dragon, Kenny's turning into a fairy, and I'm—"

I stop before revealing the baby phoenix to Blue.

A grin stretches across his face. "Ah . . . yes! *You* are playing with fire. How does it feel having that much power in the palm of your hand?"

I avoid Blue's eyes and wonder what I should say. Part of me wants to keep the phoenix a secret, but another part of me really wishes I had someone to talk to about the changes happening inside of me.

Blue nods as if he understands. "You don't have to hide anything from me, kid. I'm not going to scold you or threaten to take away your peculiar little pet. Yes— I know all about that beautiful little bird you've been hiding in your pocket." Blue pauses, and then a glimmer of mischief sparks in his eyes. "Ma knows, too."

My heart does a somersault. "She does? But— how . . ."

"She's a witch, kid. And like you just said—elders are wise. They can be cunning, too. That little bird is a source of very intense, very ancient energy. You can keep it in your pocket, but you can't hide the signal it's sending."

I think about how the egg buzzed before the phoenix was born. Was that a signal? Who was it communicating with—and why? "I just want to keep it safe," I tell Blue.

"Sure you do, kid. I think that's why you haven't told Ma—you know she won't let you keep it. Sis won't be satisfied until this world is purged of magic, and she's counting on Ma to make that happen. But you know it doesn't have to be that way."

"Is that why you changed us with that experimental gas?"

"Yes! Though I'm not sure how long the effects will last. But you and your friends represent the future, Jax. You can show the others what's possible when we embrace difference instead of punishing it by pushing it away. No one has to get hurt—in fact, just the opposite will happen. At least, that's my hypothesis. You represent the best of both our worlds, Jax, because you three are part human and part magical."

"We're mutants."

Blue grimaces. "That's such an unpleasant word! I prefer 'enhanced beings.'"

"You should have asked us first instead of treating us like lab rats," I insist.

"True. I could have asked for volunteers, but the kind of people who *want* special powers are precisely the kind of people who shouldn't have them. You three never asked for anything. You're clever, and loyal, and you work well together. That made you ideal candidates for my plan."

"Which is . . . ?"

"To show the Supreme Council—and everyone else—that they have no reason to fear magic getting into the hands of everyday humans. Your generation could be the first to bridge the two realms."

Blue stops talking, which gives me a moment to absorb everything he has said. Could my friends and I really be the future? "I need to talk to my friends. They need to know what you've done to them—to us."

"Of course. And I'm happy to answer any questions they may have. The way I see it, true friendships are built on trust. I know you think I'm the bad guy in this scenario, but have I ever lied to you, kid? I sought you out so I could tell you the truth—the whole truth. But what has Ma done? She's kept you away from the convention. Did she even tell you about the trial tomorrow?"

I don't have to answer. Blue can tell by the look on my face that Ma hasn't told me anything.

"Ask yourself *why*, Jax. It's an honor and a sacred duty to appear before the Supreme Council."

"What *is* the Supreme Council?"

"It's kind of like the magical world's Supreme Court. I filed a complaint. The members of the council reviewed it and decided it was worth holding a trial."

"Are you on trial for trying to smuggle your 'friends' out of Palmara?"

Blue shakes his head. "*I'm* not on trial, because *I* didn't break any laws. Sis did. She closed all the portals without warning and took my friends against their will. Sis thinks she's above the law, but she's not—all of us have to honor the rules set by the Supreme Council."

"Why do they want to talk to me?" I ask.

"I listed you as a witness in my complaint. You were there—you saw what Sis did."

"Yeah—she turned into a giant dragon!"

"Exactly! She crossed over and used her power to intimidate others. Then she had the nerve to lecture ME about upsetting the balance between the realms. And your grandfather helped her capture the hostages."

I frown. "Does that mean he's in trouble, too?" I don't want to say or do anything that might hurt Trub.

"No—he was just following orders. He's doing the same thing now—chasing his tail all because Sis told him to."

"What do you mean? Do you know where Trub is?"

"I'm afraid your grandfather's in a tight spot right now."

"Is he okay?" I ask, trying not to panic.

Blue sighs. "I want to help you, kid. I really do. But you know what reciprocity is, right? I need you to help me, too."

"By telling the Supreme Council what I saw that night."

Blue nods. "That's all you have to do. Tell the truth—the whole truth and nothing but the truth. If you didn't get the summons back in Brooklyn, then Ma must have intercepted it and hidden it from you. *Why?* Why would she deny you a chance to speak before our most esteemed elders?"

I hear Ma's harsh words echo in my head: "You just ain't ready to join the conversation." But what has Ma done to *make* me ready? She sealed her books so I couldn't study on my own and had me pulling up weeds at the park week after week. She wasn't even going to bring me with her to Chicago, and now that I'm here, she's avoiding me.

I feel so mixed-up right now that I can't sit still. I jump up and almost apologize to Blue. What if he really is trying to help me? Why should I be mad at Blue when Ma's the one who's been keeping secrets?

"I gotta go," I say sullenly.

Blue nods. He doesn't try to stop me or change my mind. "Sure, kid. Go home and get some rest. You got a big day tomorrow. I really hope I see you at the trial."

I head out of the park with a fire smoldering in my belly. I'm not ready to face Ma right now, so I wander around the neighborhood, trying to sort out my thoughts. Mostly I'm mad—but do I have a right to be angry with Ma? Blue is probably just trying to wind me up . . . yet most of what he said was true. Or it made sense, at least. Grown-ups *do* think they know what's best for everyone, and they never stop to ask us kids how we think or feel.

If the Supreme Council has summoned me, they must believe I have something valuable to contribute. I walk and walk until my feet start to ache. Finally, I head back to the rooming house. My mind is made up. I *am* going to the trial tomorrow morning. Whether Ma likes it or not, I *am* going to testify.

10

I run into Miss Ellabelle as soon as I turn the corner onto our block. She scowls at me and reaches into her purse for a large, old-fashioned key. "Here—take this. I can't keep the ladies in my club waiting any longer. You'll have to let yourself in and fix yourself a sandwich in the kitchen. Clean up after yourself and stay in your room until Ma and the others return. They phoned to let me know they'd be home late this evening."

"Did they say why?" I ask.

Miss Ellabelle glances at the watch on her bony wrist and hurries down the block without bothering to answer my question. I don't mind. I don't really feel like company right now, and being alone in the house will make it easier for me to call Vik and Kenny. I have to let them know what's happening to us.

I turn the antique key in the lock and let myself into

the rooming house. The parlor doors are wide open, and Miss Ellabelle has left three stained glass lamps on. They fill the dark room with circles of warm light and make the creaky, shadowy house feel less creepy.

I remember to take off my shoes before heading down the long hall that leads to the kitchen. Just a few months ago I followed another light down a dark hallway until I reached Ma's kitchen. She made me a peanut butter sandwich and told me to mind my business when I asked her about the box from Madagascar. Then the squirrel scratched at the window, I let her into the kitchen, and everything about my life changed.

I sigh and swipe at the light switch on the wall, almost hoping to find Ma standing at the counter. She isn't there to grumble at me, of course. There's no squirrel at the window and no box of baby dragons on the table. It's just an ordinary room, but I am no longer an ordinary boy.

The kitchen in the rooming house is much bigger than the one in Ma's apartment. Everything is white, from the tiles on the floor to the marble countertops. The cabinets and the tiled walls are all spotless—scrubbed clean by Miss Ellabelle and daring a boy like me to leave a stain. I pull another granola bar from my bag and munch on it instead of making myself a sandwich. I take out my phone and see a missed call from Kenny. I'm not sure how to explain that we're mutants now, but I go ahead and call him back.

Kenny's voice booms in my ear. "Jax—is that you? Perfect timing! Vik's here—Kavi, too."

"I wish you were here. I really miss all of you," I say, surprised by the way my voice catches in my throat. Is it getting harder to tell the truth? Or is this another way the phoenix is changing me? I'm a witch's apprentice. My friends look up to me—envy me, even. What would they think if they saw the tears shining in my eyes?

"Are you okay, Jax?" Kenny asks.

I sigh and climb onto one of the stools that are evenly spaced along the wall. There's no table, which is probably Miss Ellabelle's way of discouraging guests from lingering in her too-cold, too-clean kitchen. I rest my elbow on the counter and sigh again. "I'm just tired. It's been a really long day."

"I want to hear all about Chicago," Kenny says excitedly, "but let's do this with video! Hang on a second, Jax."

Kenny sets the phone down. I hear him open the metal cabinet in his backyard shed. That's where Kenny keeps all his snacks, but the box he moves from the cabinet to the table sounds heavy.

Vik picks up the phone while his little sister helps Kenny with the box.

"Hey, Jax. How's the phoenix?"

"I think it's okay," I tell him, "except it sleeps a lot. And I worry that it's cold. Is it supposed to shiver so much?"

"Beats me," Vik says. "I'd expect a phoenix to keep itself warm. Do you have an electric heater? That might be a quick way to warm the bird up. Or a blow dryer—do any of your witches have one?"

"Hang on—let me see what I can find."

I set the phone down and think about the giant fireplace in the front room. Miss Ellabelle would pitch a fit if she came home and found a fire—and a phoenix—burning in her private parlor. Then I glance over at the stove. It's stainless steel and has six burners instead of four like our stove at home. I'm not allowed to cook unless there's an adult with me in the kitchen. I think about what Blue said earlier about all the rules adults make up to keep kids from doing what they want to do.

"I'll just turn it on and keep the flame low," I tell myself. My heart speeds up as I turn the dial, wait for the clicking sound, and then watch the flame leap up around the front burner. The phoenix chirps happily and settles on the metal grill that would normally hold a pot above the flame. I turn the dial down as low as it will go and hope that will keep it warm.

When I pick the phone up again, I hear a commotion in the background. "What's Kenny up to?" I ask.

Vik laughs as he describes the scene inside Kenny's shed. "He's got a big box full of presents from his dad— and he hasn't opened half of them!"

In the background I hear paper being torn. Kavita giggles, so I assume she's helping Kenny unwrap some of his gifts.

"My dad sent me a tablet for my birthday last year," Kenny explains. "He said it would help us stay in touch, but he never calls. Glad I didn't chuck it, though. How's it work?"

I hear Kavita say, "Give it to me."

Vik objects. "You don't know what you're doing, Kavi. Let me see it."

"I know exactly what to do, Vikram. Stop being so bossy!"

I remind Vik that it's probably not a good idea to quarrel with his little sister right now. He sighs and says, "Let me call you back, Jax."

Fifteen minutes go by before my phone rings again. I turn my camera on and see my three friends huddled together in the shed. Vik is sitting at the table, and his sister is standing right behind him, peering at the screen over his shoulder. At first, I can see half of Kenny's face. Then he disappears, and all I see is . . . his knees!

There's a moment of chaos, and the tablet falls over. When it's upright once more, they've switched positions. Kenny is seated at the table with Vik and Kavita standing on either side him. Each of them has a hand clamped on Kenny's shoulder, and I realize they're holding him in place.

"Can you really fly, Kenny?"

"Uh . . . not exactly. Not yet, at least. It's hard when I don't have wings. Mostly I just hover."

"He's like a balloon filled with helium. Maybe we should tie him to the chair," Kavita says with a smile.

"That's not funny, Kavi," Vik snaps.

But it is *kind of* funny, and Kenny chuckles along with me. It feels good to share a joke with my friends. "I've got so much to tell you. I don't even know where to begin."

"Why don't you start by telling us about the convention," Kenny suggests. "How many witches have you met?"

"Just the three in Ma's coven who took the UR with us—Dutch, Quayesha, and Mrs. Benjamin."

"What's the 'er'?" Kavi asks.

I decide to give the short version. "It's basically a sturdy bubble that travels underground. It wasn't working properly, but we still got here in no time. I think the phoenix egg might have made the UR malfunction."

Kavi's eyes grow wide. "Phoenix egg?"

I look at Vik, and he gives a slight nod. "Your brother found it last summer and gave it to me to protect." I don't mention that Kavi is the reason Vik wanted to get the egg out of his house.

"Have you told Ma about it yet?" Vik asks.

I sigh and shake my head. "Not yet. But Blue said she already knows. Apparently, the phoenix emits some kind of signal."

Kenny makes a face and says, "Blue? What's that creep doing in Chicago?"

"Has he kidnapped any other magical creatures?" Kavi asks, still bitter about the way Blue treated Mo. Then she folds her arms across her chest and directs her anger at us. "How come no one else is curious about the phoenix? Did everyone know about it except me? I hate secrets!"

Kenny looks at Vik. Vik looks at me.

"Actually . . . your brother asked me to show it to Ma, so I brought it with me to Chicago. And then yesterday, it hatched!"

"Can I see it? Please, please, please!" Kavi cries with her hands clasped.

"Stop being such a pest, Kavi! Jax doesn't have time for show-and-tell," Vik says impatiently. "We've got important things to discuss."

"I don't mind," I say, but before I can turn my phone to show the little phoenix perched on the stove, Kavita *snarls* at Vik.

He holds out his hand and tries to calm her down, but Kavita has already started to transform. Two threads of smoke come out of her nostrils, and her lizard eyes flash with rage.

"Kavi, NO!" Vik tries to be firm with her, but it's clear that he's scared. He backs away from his snarling sister and pleads, "Not here—not now!"

Kenny jumps up and flings open the doors of his metal cabinet. He starts to float again but still manages to grab a bag of marshmallows and offer it to Kavita. Her eyes dim, and a smile creeps across her face as she greedily snatches the plastic bag from Kenny's hand.

"Um—why don't you eat them outside?" Kenny suggests.

Kavita nods and walks out the door Vik is holding open for her.

"Whew—that was close! Quick thinking, Kenny," I tell him. "How long does it take for her to go back to her normal self again?"

"No time at all," Vik says. He turns the tablet so I can see his little sister sitting on the grass, shoving fistfuls of powdery white marshmallows into her mouth.

Kenny closes the door and then disappears from view. I hear him muttering and fumbling with—or bumping into—the tools that hang on the wall of the shed. Then he appears again, and I smile as I realize that Kenny has taken Kavi's advice and tied himself to the leg of the table.

Gripping the tabletop with his hands to steady himself, Kenny says, "So tell us about your encounter with Blue."

I take a deep breath and begin. "Uh . . . my friend Vonn took me to him. Blue told me he's taking Sis to court, and he wants me to testify tomorrow."

"Wow. And you're okay with that? *Ma's* okay with that?" Vik asks.

"Apparently not," I grumble. "She hid the summons sent to me by the Supreme Council! They want to hear my point of view, but Ma hasn't even mentioned the trial. And she hasn't let me go to the convention with her, either."

Kenny frowns. "So what have you been doing for the past couple of days?"

"Learning about the city and taking care of the

phoenix," I tell him. "Then Blue told me about the trial, and . . . well, he told me something else that you need to know. That night when we were inside the emporium, we breathed in some type of gas. That's what's making us change."

"Speak for yourself," Vik says. "Nothing's happening to me."

I hear a tinge of envy in Vik's voice and hurry to explain that the changes are temporary. "Blue said the effects wouldn't last. He just wants to prove that humans and magical creatures can coexist peacefully in our world."

"But can they?" Vik asks doubtfully. "There's been nothing but chaos at home since Kavi started turning into a dragon. Kenny has to hide out in his shed and tie himself down so he doesn't float away. This is all my fault!"

"You're not responsible for any of this, Vik," I insist. "Blue set a trap for us, and we walked right into it."

"But we only went there to save my sister," Vik says quietly.

"And the dragon."

"And your aunt," Kenny adds.

"The point is, we were trying to do the right thing," I remind Vik. "Blue counts on kids like us wanting to prove ourselves and not let anyone else down. That's why his sleeping spell only affects adults. He figures the world could be a lot better if the older generations let us run things for a while."

"Sounds good to me," Kenny says. "Adults have messed everything up. They break their promises and fight all the time—and just look at the environment. We may not have fresh air or clean water when we grow up!"

"Adults aren't perfect, that's for sure," I admit. "They expect us to be honest and tell the truth, but they don't always set a good example."

For a moment none of us speak as we think about the grown-ups who have let us down. Vik is the first to say something.

"So, do you have special powers now, too?" Vik asks.

I nod but decide not to tell him about the three bullies. "I haven't really figured out how to use them yet. I feel like Peter Parker—'With great power . . .'"

Kenny and Vik finish my sentence for me: "'. . . comes great responsibility.'"

"Right. Plus, Vonn told me that you don't have to have magic to help people. I helped someone today just by pulling up weeds in the park! It's your intention that matters most."

I'm not sure if that makes Vik feel any better, but

suddenly we're all distracted by the sound of Kavita's raised voice.

"Aunty? Aunty, is that you? Vikram—Vik, come quick!"

Vik flings open the shed door and grabs his sister by the shoulders. "Kavi—calm down! You know you can't get excited! It's too risky."

Kenny's tied to the table, so he can't follow Vik outside, but he holds the tablet up so I can see what's happening.

Kavita slaps her brother's hands away, jumps up, and insists, "But I heard her! It was Aunty—I'm positive."

"That's impossible, Kavi. I know how much you miss Aunty but . . ."

Kavi stamps her foot and puts her hands on her hips. "It's true, Vikram! I was just sitting here eating the last marshmallow, and suddenly I heard her say, 'Bau lobhi na bano!'"

"'Bau lobhi na bano'?"

Kenny's holding the tablet toward the two siblings so I can't see him, but I can hear the awe in his voice.

"Whoa . . . is that dragon-tongue?"

Kavi rolls her eyes. Vik laughs and says, "No, Kenny, it's Gujarati. Kavi heard our aunt say, 'Don't be so greedy.'"

"Come back inside—quick. I need to tell you something," Kenny says sheepishly.

They file back into the shed and gather around the table once more. Kenny props up the tablet but doesn't say anything. Vik and I look at him expectantly. When Kenny doesn't go on, Kavi grows impatient.

"Well? What's so important?"

Kenny's cheeks turn red, and Kavi looks away, ashamed at her outburst. She doesn't apologize but keeps quiet so that Kenny can share his news when he's ready.

"It's possible Kavi really did hear her aunt because, well . . . I think I got a message from Jef," Kenny says finally.

"How?" I ask.

Kenny shrugs. "I've never heard Jef's voice—none of us has. But I'm pretty sure he's trying to tell me something."

"What did he say?" Vik asks.

Kenny takes a deep breath and says, " 'Beware the crow!' "

Kavi looks disappointed. "That's it?"

Kenny nods. "That's it."

"And why do you think this message came from Jef?" Vik asks.

"It's hard to explain," Kenny tells him. "At first, I just saw letters in my head—but not the alphabet I know.

It was another language, I think. You know that it's hard for me to put letters in the right order sometimes 'cause I have dyslexia."

"We know. And yet you're the one who read the sign outside the spice factory last spring," I remind him. "Vik and I couldn't have done that without you. So maybe . . ."

"Maybe you have a gift, Kenny," Kavi says with a smile.

Kenny blushes again, but this time he doesn't stare at the floor. He looks right at me and says, "I'm pretty sure the letters I saw were from the fairy alphabet. The letters made words that I shouldn't be able to read—but I could. I think Jef is trying to warn us."

"About a crow?" Vik asks skeptically.

"Maybe Aunty's trying to warn us, too," Kavita says.

"Maybe she doesn't want you to get a mouth full of cavities from eating so many sweets," Vik mutters.

I think for a moment and realize Kavita could be right. "Wait a second—that actually makes sense. Kavi isn't bound to your aunt. The three of us have a connection to the creatures we care for. Maybe the voice you heard wasn't speaking to you, Kavi. Maybe your aunt was speaking to Mo!"

Suddenly, I smell smoke! I look over at the stove and find the little phoenix doing a strange dance around the front burner. As it moves in a circle, it whips its long tail feathers—sending a shower of sparks over the tea towel hanging from the oven door. It smolders, filling the kitchen with smoke and setting off the fire alarm. Then more sparks land on the roll of paper towels on the counter, and it bursts into flames!

"Oh no! Guys—I have to go!" I shout before dropping my phone and rushing over to the phoenix. Alarmed, it flaps its wings and lifts off the grill over the burner. I turn the gas off, but the phoenix continues to send sparks all over the kitchen. I cough and search for a fire extinguisher but ultimately settle for a cup filled with water from the sink. I throw it at the paper towel roll, but that just makes even more smoke. It's getting hard to see in the kitchen, and the smoke alarm is beeping so loudly that my ears ache.

I can hear the panicked voices coming down the hall, though, so I splash more water on the burning tail feathers and tuck the phoenix inside my hoodie. Then I prepare myself to face Miss Ellabelle's rage. Instead, Dutch rushes in with a silk kerchief pressed against her mouth. She holds out her hand so that it looks like a spider, and a plume of white foam sprays over the counter and the stove. Quayesha leads me out of the kitchen and parks me in the front foyer. Then she returns to the kitchen to help Dutch silence the angry alarm.

I anxiously peer out the front window, fearing that Ma and Mrs. Benjamin will walk in on the chaos I created. Relieved to find the street empty, I unzip my hoodie to check on the phoenix. It looks up at me with sad eyes. "It's not your fault," I tell it. "I should have watched what you were doing. It's dangerous to play with fire." The damp little bird shivers, so I zip up my hoodie to keep it warm. Then I creep back down the hallway and stick my head into the kitchen. Dutch is still holding out her hand, but this time there's no foam—she has created a sort of vacuum that's sucking up all the soot and foam and water. Quayesha seems to have opened a window and created a gale that draws out the smoke and fills the kitchen with fresh air. I watch them work wordlessly and, for just a moment, wish they had been tasked with training me instead of Ma.

"That was amazing," I say breathlessly.

Quayesha and Dutch nod at each other and then both turn to look at me. "Don't tell Ma, okay?"

I'm in no rush to reveal the mess I've made—if they hadn't returned at just the right moment, the fire could have spread. "You two are lifesavers! I could have burned down the whole house. I definitely won't be bragging about that," I assure them.

"What happened?" Dutch asks.

"Um—I wanted to make something warm to eat, so I turned on the stove. . . ." I look around and spot my dad's phone on the floor. I rush over to pick it up. "But then my phone rang and it was my friends back in Brooklyn. They had an emergency, too, and I was try-ing to help them. . . ." I hang my head and add, "I guess

I took my eye off the stove. I'm really sorry—it won't happen again."

"Where's the pot?" Quayesha asks skeptically.

"What pot?"

"You said you were cooking. I assume you weren't holding the food over an open fire."

I blink and try to think of an answer. Dutch saves me by pulling a folded brochure from her pocket.

"You still hungry, Junior?" Dutch asks. "We were thinking about ordering in. Or maybe trying that chicken-and-waffles joint up the block."

My stomach grumbles softly at the mention of food, but I decide I'd better keep the phoenix safe in my room from now on.

"You two go ahead. I think I'll just take a bath and go to bed. I've had enough excitement for one day."

Quayesha gives me a strange look, but Dutch just nods and heads down the hallway. I hear the front door shut behind her.

Quayesha opens her mouth to speak, but I manage to ask my own question first. "Why don't you want Ma to know that you saved me—and the house?"

She looks around the spotless kitchen and sighs. "Ma's old school. She and Mrs. B. think witches should only use their powers when we're on a mission. Lots of witches use their magic for everyday things—like vacuuming or doing the dishes. Others set up shop and sell their services. There's plenty of demand for potions and predictions. But Ma doesn't think witches should use their magic to make money or to make life easier for ourselves."

I sigh and say, "I wish I could learn how to do what you did tonight, but Ma says I'm not ready to cast spells."

"Well, magic is a big responsibility," Quayesha replies. "Lots of people want power, but they don't always know what to do with it."

Her words make me think of Spider-Man. Quayesha could go on, but she stops and looks at the shiny steel stovetop instead. I finish her thought for her by saying, "I guess I just proved that I'm not the most responsible person in the world."

Quayesha puts her hand on my shoulder and gives it a squeeze. "We all make mistakes, Jax. That's how we learn."

I do my best to smile before heading down the hall that leads to the staircase.

Quayesha follows me and asks, "You sure you're not hungry? Dutch won't be long."

I shake my head and start up the creaky stairs. "I better call my mom and then get some rest. I think tomorrow's going to be a big day."

11

In the morning I feed the phoenix another piece of gum and then tuck it into the towel before heading downstairs. Everyone is seated at the dining room table, and instead of slimy gray gruel, they're digging into platters piled high with crisp bacon, fluffy pancakes, buttered toast, and scrambled eggs.

I say good morning and take a seat across the table from Ma. I've been rehearsing my speech ever since I woke up and hope I have the courage to say it to her face. But Ma pays me no mind. Like the others, she's too busy eating breakfast and arguing with Mrs. Benjamin about the best way to reverse the sleeping spell.

"Ahem." Dutch, who's sitting next to me, glances my way, but nobody else pays any attention to me. I clear my throat again, louder this time.

Quayesha also frowns at me from her seat at the end of the table. "You feeling okay, Jax?"

I nod and nervously nibble on a piece of toast. Then I take a deep breath and—with my eyes on Ma—say, "I saw Blue yesterday."

The room instantly goes quiet as everyone stops eating and talking. All eyes are on me, but it's Ma I speak to. I feel like she's seeing me for the first time in a long time. Now that I've finally got her attention, I have to make this moment count.

I grip the edge of my seat with both hands to stop them from trembling. "Blue told me about the trial. He told me the Supreme Council summoned me to testify, but I never received anything. Why?"

Mrs. Benjamin loudly sucks her teeth. "That worthless man lies every time he opens his mouth. You can't see his forked tongue?"

I ignore Mrs. Benjamin and keep my gaze locked on Ma. "Blue said to ask you about the trial. That's why you're really here, right? And that's why you won't let me go with you to the convention. You don't want me to testify against Sis."

Ma wipes her mouth with her napkin and then calmly folds it and sets it next to her plate. "What's Rule #2, Jax?"

"Trust your elders," I reply. "But why should I trust you when you haven't been telling me the truth? Rules aren't just for kids like me. You hid the summons from me—isn't that against the rules? Sis took all those creatures back to Palmara without their consent. That's against the rules, too."

"That's not what happened," Ma says in a low voice.

"How would you know?" I ask. "You weren't even there! But *I* was—and that's why the Supreme Council wants *me* to testify." I pause to take a deep breath before adding, "And that's why I'm going to the trial."

Ma frowns and turns to her fellow witches. "Could you all give us a moment alone?"

Dutch grabs a couple of strips of bacon, picks up her plate, and pushes back from the table. Quayesha's about to do the same, but I blurt out, "No! Let them stay. We're a coven, right? We shouldn't have any secrets. We should all be on the same page, since we're *supposed* to be on the same side."

Dutch and Quayesha exchange surprised looks before turning to Ma. She keeps her eyes on me but nods once, and everyone sits back down.

"Blue probably made a lot of claims," she begins, "and I bet some of them even made sense. But he's just using you, Jax. He wants you to say things that will help his cause. He doesn't care about you."

I shrug. "I don't need him to care about me. I have friends—true friends—and family members who love me. Blue respects me enough to tell me what's really going on. You only tell me what you want me to know. You keep saying I'm not ready to learn more, but I am! You just want to keep all the power for yourself. But you know what? That's fine by me 'cause I got my own power. I've got a voice, and I'm going to use it."

"No, you're not."

Ma speaks softly, even though everyone can tell how mad she is right now. The hair on the back of my neck stands up, but I won't back down—not when I know I'm right. "You can't stop me," I say defiantly.

"I can and I will."

Ma presses her lips together, but I still hear a faint chant coming from inside her mouth. Or is it inside my head?

Quayesha looks distressed. "Ma, don't . . . please."

Dutch backs her up by adding, "I'm sure Junior didn't mean it. He's just a kid."

At first, I don't understand why they're pleading with Ma. Then I try to get up from the table and realize . . .

that I can't. It's like I'm glued to the chair—and the chair is bolted to the floor! I glare at Ma and feel a small fire smoldering deep in my belly.

"Let . . . me . . . go." I manage to keep my voice low, even though I feel anything but calm right now. I wait for the fire to spread through my body like it did yesterday, but instead, the flame wavers and grows dim.

Ma snorts, amused. "Not so strong after all, huh? Not when your fiery friend isn't tucked inside your pocket."

My eyes open wide, and Ma laughs again.

"Oh, I know all about that baby bird. You see, Jax, what you fail to realize is, getting old has its advantages. There's not much I haven't seen or heard or done in my lifetime. And here you are, not even ten years old, trying to tell ME what to do."

I strain against the spell, but it won't let me move. "You can do whatever you want," I tell Ma, "but you can't decide what's right for me—not anymore! From now on, I make my own decisions, and I choose to go to the trial."

Ma pushes her chair back and stands up. "I don't think so."

Mrs. Benjamin dabs at her mouth with a napkin before standing as well. "You're leaving him here?"

"Might as well," Ma replies. "I'm sure Miss Ellabelle will keep an eye on him. Makes it easy for her to feed him when he's already at the table."

"LET—ME—GO!" I holler, and for just a moment, the fire inside of me flares back to life. I struggle against Ma's spell, but she must know it's futile because Ma pats me on the head as she walks by. Quayesha and Dutch exchange worried glances and silently agree to stage another protest.

Quayesha plants herself in the doorway so that Ma has to stop and listen to her. "Jax has learned his lesson, Ma. Reverse the spell—please."

"At least let Junior stay in his room," Dutch says.

Ma shakes her head, and Quayesha tries another approach. "Then let him come with us today. I promise I'll keep an eye on him. He can observe the trial—nothing more."

Dutch nods enthusiastically. "We all know the Supreme Council is going to throw out Blue's complaint. Why not let Junior see how the system works? It would do him good to hear you testify."

Ma is unmoved by their appeals. "He's not ready," she says stubbornly.

"Yes, I am!" I shout as I struggle pointlessly against her spell.

"The boy clearly has no self-control," Mrs. Benjamin says with obvious disdain.

Quayesha pushes past her and puts a protective hand on my shoulder. "Release him, Ma. I know Jax will be on his best behavior. Won't you, Jax?"

I appreciate Quayesha standing up for me, but I'm not sure I can live up to her expectations. I'm going to the trial no matter what. But I can't say that out loud, which means I have to lie. I feel the pressure of everyone watching me, so I just hang my head and nod silently.

Ma studies me longer than the rest. I can tell she's not sure she can trust me, but finally, she relents. I hear the same whispering voice in my head, and in an instant I'm unbound. I push my chair back and stand up. My legs and arms tingle as if my limbs have fallen asleep. I take a step toward the dining room door and nearly topple over. Dutch and Quayesha catch me and help me stay upright.

"Go to your room and stay there," Ma says gruffly. "I'll deal with you when I get back tonight."

Quayesha sighs. "His room's tiny, Ma."

My room is the only place I want to be right now, but Dutch agrees with Quayesha. "You can't keep the kid cooped up all day. At least let him play in the backyard. . . ."

"Absolutely not," Ma says. "With that baby phoenix,

he's a hazard to himself and to others. Either I take the bird or he keeps it but stays in his room. Those are the only options."

"Why?" Quayesha asks, exasperated by Ma's stubbornness.

"BECAUSE I SAID SO!"

Ma's booming voice catches all of us by surprise. Quayesha folds her arms across her chest and twists her lips into a knot to stop herself from saying anything else. Dutch helps me walk over to the staircase. Once I grab hold of the banister, I slowly climb the stairs on my wobbly legs. Behind me I hear the witches still arguing about me in the dining room.

"You wouldn't treat any other member of the coven that way."

"He's not a witch—the boy is *my* apprentice, and I'll deal with him as I see fit."

"Jax is one of us. . . ."

"He's *not!*" Ma barks.

I stop on the staircase and wait for Mrs. Benjamin to say something salty, but she doesn't even suck her teeth. Instead, she sighs heavily and says, "The boy does not belong at the trial because he does not belong in our coven. I have consulted the bones. He is not destined to become one of us."

"But—"

The hard edge returns to Mrs. Benjamin's voice. "Enough, girl! Wanting something to be true does not make it so."

I almost turn around. I even open my mouth to object, but something inside of me knows that Mrs. Benjamin is right. Still, as mad as I am right now, hearing that truth said out loud brings tears to my eyes. I blink quickly to clear my vision and continue climbing the stairs. The bison on the wall above watches me, shaking its woolly head sympathetically.

It takes me a while to reach the second-floor landing, and by that time, the witches are gathered in the foyer. I hear Ma say, "Make sure he's in his room. I'll tell Miss E. he's not to leave the house today."

I hear Ma shuffle down the hall toward the kitchen and expect to hear footsteps behind me on the stairs. But no one comes up after me, and by the time I finally reach my room, the tears I was holding back are falling freely. I flop onto the bed and wrap my arms around the warm nest of the sleeping phoenix. My tears soak into the towel, and before I know it, I'm asleep. I wake to the sound of my phone buzzing in my back pocket. I pull it out and see there's a text message from Quayesha.

U OK?

NO.

U MAD?

It's not fair.

I KNOW. YOU STILL WANT TO GO TO THE TRIAL?

YES! Can you help me?

The screen shows that Quayesha is writing something, but after several seconds, no new message appears. I wait a moment and wonder if I should text her again to thank her for sticking up for me at breakfast. Then the dots appear again, and I hope this time her message comes through.

OPEN THE CLOSET.

I stare at the screen and wonder if Quayesha meant to text that message to someone else. There isn't even a closet in my bedroom. There's just a small square door that opens into the shaft that used to house the dumbwaiter. Back in the day, servants used pulleys and a wooden tray to move things upstairs and downstairs more easily. There's nothing there but air now—I know because I checked yesterday.

Quayesha must know I have my doubts, because she texts me again.

JUST DO IT, JAX.

I carefully get up from the bed so I don't wake the sleeping phoenix. It only takes three steps for me to cross the room, and so within seconds the dumbwaiter door is wide open—and so is my mouth!

Yesterday there was a brick wall draped with cobwebs staring back at me, but today there is an endless plain covered in golden grass. The sky is so vast it is barely blue and there's not a tree in sight. There is something dark in the distance, so I lean into the square doorway to get a better look. Soon the black mass becomes more defined, and I can tell that it's a pack of animals. One large creature leaves the herd, and soon I see that it has horns and a shaggy mane—it's a bison!

"Hello, friend," it says as it nears the dumbwaiter door.

"Hello. How . . . are you . . . ?" I can't think of anything else to say. I imagine how I must look from the bison's point of view—much like a boy whose head is mounted on a wooden plaque. Then I realize that's exactly what's happened! Somehow the house has turned inside out. When the bison downstairs pulls its head out of the wall, this must be where it goes.

The bison nods at me as if to confirm my thoughts. "You brought ancient magic back into this old house, which released me. In exchange, I have brought you the key you seek."

"The key?" As far as I know, the door to my bedroom isn't locked. Why would I need a key?

"The room you wish to enter is sealed with magic. Opening it will require the assistance of true friends."

I think for a moment. The room I wish to enter is the courtroom of the Supreme Council. The only thing that's stopping me from going to the trial is the fact that I don't even know where it's being held.

The bison nods once more before stepping aside to reveal . . . Quayesha! She's not wearing what she had on this morning. She shimmers in the grassy field, and I blink to bring her into focus, but it doesn't work. The wind makes the grass move like a golden sea, but nothing on Quayesha's body moves—not her locks or the hem of her flowing dress.

"Are you really there?" I ask.

Quayesha steps closer to the dumbwaiter door. "Is that better?"

Her voice sounds staticky, and she still wavers a bit, but I can see her face more clearly now. "Where are you?"

"At the trial," she replies. "I don't have long, and Ma won't forgive me for doing this but . . ." Quayesha glances over her shoulder before adding, "I don't care what anyone says. You have a right to be here, Jax."

She pulls out her phone and taps the screen with her long diamond-tipped nail. No messages appear on my phone's screen, so I figure she must be calling someone else. Quayesha holds the phone up to her ear, and her locks fall across her face as she speaks to whoever's on the other end. I try to hear what she's saying, but within seconds the call ends, and Quayesha pulls back her veil of hair.

"There's a park not too far from here—it's on Calumet and Forty-Fourth. Think you can find your way over there?" she asks.

"Sure. Why?"

"Vonn's going to meet you there in fifteen minutes."

"Can he get me into the trial?"

Quayesha shrugs. "If Vonn can't, no one can."

Then she slides her phone into the pocket of her dress and waves before fading from view.

"Thanks, Quayesha," I call out.

The bison stops grazing and comes so close that I could reach out and touch its regal mane if I dared. That seems disrespectful, though, so I just smile appreciatively and say, "Thank you for connecting us."

"Close the door and seal the worlds once more. Take the dumbwaiter down to the basement. The cellar door will let you into the yard, and you can make your way to the street undetected. Good luck, friend."

I look into its beautiful black eyes and say, "Thank you for everything . . . friend."

The bison turns and heads across the never-ending field to rejoin the herd. I close the dumbwaiter door and use my phone to find the location of the park. The app shows a small park that's less than ten minutes away. All I have to do is pack the phoenix in my bag and get down to the basement.

The drowsy bird doesn't object when I wrap it in the towel and place it inside my book bag. I slip my arms through the straps and take a deep breath. As instructed, I open the dumbwaiter door and find the bison was right—once again there's a brick shaft full of cobwebs. I reach for the closest rope, and after a few tugs, a wooden platform appears. It's meant to hold clean laundry or a tray of food, but I'm hoping it will hold my weight.

I crawl into the shaft and pull the door shut behind me. Then I lower myself down to the basement, going slowly at first before losing hold of the rope and landing with a loud bang. Luckily, there's no one to hear me besides a few mice that skitter into the shadows. I fling open the cellar door and climb up the stairs leading into the sunny backyard. Above me I can hear Miss Ellabelle talking to someone on the phone.

"Now, Mabel, you know I'm not one to gossip, and all guests have their own peculiarities. But these witches are just impossible to predict! This time they showed up with a *boy* of all things and expected me to just look the other way. Well, I don't know what he's gone and done, but the little ruffian is confined to his room for the rest of the day. I was told to take his meals upstairs and not let him leave the house under any circumstance. It really is *too much....*"

I almost wish Miss Ellabelle could see me escaping right under her nose! But to be on the safe side, I skirt the house, staying close to the wall so she doesn't look out the window and see me. Then I dash across the front yard, let myself out the cast-iron gate, and head up the block to Forty-Fourth Street.

The park isn't hard to find, but it's empty except for a couple of mothers who stand and chat while their kids play on the jungle gym. To pass the time, I wander along the paved path and find a plaque explaining that the park is named after Hadiya Pendleton, a girl from the neighborhood who wasn't much older than me when she was killed by gunfire. I think about what Blue said last spring—that Sis could make the world better with magic, but she chooses instead to let bad things happen. At the time, Sis's explanation made sense to me, but now I've got my own magical powers. What if the bullies who picked on Itzel yesterday had had a gun? What could I have done to help her then?

Just as I check the time on my phone, I spot Vonn sitting on the back of a park bench, his sneakered feet planted where his butt should be. Today he's wearing pants, a T-shirt, and a coat all in khaki camouflage print, making me wonder if that's why I didn't spot him at first. He's munching on something, and when I get close, Vonn holds out the paper bag to offer me some. I didn't really get to eat breakfast, so I reach into the bag and pull out a handful of orange and brown popcorn.

Vonn tosses some into his own mouth and says, "Garrett's Mix is the breakfast of champions."

I'm not sure what to expect, but after munching the strange mix for a while, I realize the cheese and caramel flavors actually taste really good together. Vonn hands me the bag as I climb up beside him on the bench.

"Quay tells me you had some trouble on the home front this morning," Vonn says. "Thought it was odd when Ma told me not to come by."

"I'd still be stuck in my room if it weren't for Quayesha. She's a true friend—and so are you. Thanks for helping me get into the trial, Vonn."

"You sure you wanna do this, Brooklyn?" Vonn asks. "Disobeying your boss isn't generally a good idea."

"I know. But Ma's not really my boss anymore. Mrs. Benjamin said I'm not part of their coven and that's why I don't belong at the trial. But I have to go— I was summoned by the Supreme Council."

Vonn nods. "I get that you want to have your say, but I'm sure I don't have to tell you that our choices have consequences. Ma might see this as a betrayal."

I think about that for a moment. It *does* feel like I'm switching sides. Then I remember how angry I felt when Ma used her binding spell to keep me stuck in my chair back at the rooming house. Why should I feel a way about letting down someone who has already betrayed me? I decide to ask Vonn for his opinion. "Do you think I should testify?"

I'm expecting him to say something deep, but Vonn just shrugs and says, "We all have a role to play."

Vonn's been around for hundreds of years and I haven't even lived a whole decade. Maybe the Supreme Council should be listening to Vonn instead of me. But he's not the one who witnessed what Sis did that night back in Brooklyn. It was me.

"If you were in my position, what would you do?" I ask Vonn.

"If someone wanted to know what I thought, I'd speak up. I'd use my words to fight for the world I want to live in." Vonn eases himself off the bench and brushes traces of popcorn off his khaki ensemble. "Ready?" he asks.

"Ready," I reply, hopping off the bench. I offer Vonn the rest of the popcorn, but he tells me to keep it. I roll the paper bag shut and unzip my knapsack. The phoenix pokes its head out and chirps at me. I transfer it to my pocket, pack the popcorn, and sling my bag over my shoulder.

"Follow me," Vonn says as we take the path that leads out of the park.

12

It looks like we're heading to the L, but Vonn stops before reaching the stairs that lead up to the train's platform. Instead, he takes me over to an old brick building that's clearly under construction. There's scaffolding all along the front, and the entrance is boarded up with plywood. Torn sheets of black plastic cover the tall windows, and trash has gathered along the curb. Weeds poke up from the cracks in the sidewalk, and the elevated tracks rumble as a train pulls out of the station next door.

Near the top of the pointed roof is a small round window, and beneath that is a smooth stone block with the words THE FORUM chiseled into it. People walk past the building, but no one stops to read the posters that plaster the walls. This place might have been important once, but it's clear this building hasn't been a destination in a long time.

I look at the three arched windows on the building's facade and ask, "Was this a church once?"

Vonn shakes his head. "The Forum is one of the oldest assembly halls in Chicago. Folks gathered here for concerts and lectures. Every important meeting happened here back in the day."

"Okay, but why are we here now?" I ask, trying to hide my impatience. I don't want to miss my chance to see the Supreme Council.

"Thought you said you wanted to check out the trial."

I look from Vonn to the dilapidated building before us. "THIS is where the witch convention is being held? I thought it was at the convention center downtown."

Vonn shakes his head. "Our kind prefers to keep a low profile. We keep ourselves to ourselves, if you know what I mean."

"I get that, but . . . couldn't they find a nicer place to meet?"

Vonn grins. "What you know 'bout glamour, Brooklyn?"

"Glamour? Not much. My mom likes to watch movie stars wearing their fancy clothes on the red carpet. Is that what you mean?"

"Kind of. Sometimes the clothes a person puts on can disguise who they really are inside. But when it comes to magic, glamour is a type of spell that makes something ugly or just ordinary look dope. The illusion's so good you think it's real."

I take another look at the Forum. "So . . . this building just *looks* like a dump?"

"See for yourself." Vonn leads me around to the back of the Forum. He pries off a loose sheet of plywood that's been nailed over the door. We squeeze through and find ourselves in a dark room that smells musty. The carpet squishes beneath my feet, and I think I hear mice squeaking and scurrying around. Vonn takes out his phone and turns on the light. I do the same, and after a moment my eyes get used to the dark.

"Watch your step," Vonn warns me.

I avoid the broken milk crates and soggy cardboard boxes that litter the floor as I follow him over to a wide staircase. When I grip the railing, it pulls free from the wall. I stagger backward, but Vonn quickly turns to grab hold of my arm.

"You good, Brooklyn?" he asks.

"I'm good," I say as I steady myself.

Vonn turns back around and continues climbing the stairs. I follow him, casting the light from my phone over the walls. The gilded sconces once had dangling tear-shaped crystals, but most are broken or covered in a thick coat of dust. Layers of mismatched paint and water-stained wallpaper peel away to reveal cratered, crumbling plaster. When we reach the top of the staircase, Vonn points to a stage at the far end of the hall. The high-ceilinged room is so cavernous that our voices echo, even though we're whispering.

It's cool and dank in the empty ballroom. I shiver and glance up at the three arched windows high above us. The torn plastic covering the broken glass flutters as wind whistles in from outside. Once upon a time, the Forum must have been a fancy place to meet, but not anymore. "There's nothing glamorous about this place," I whisper to myself.

"Wait here," Vonn says.

I do as I'm told and watch as he moves through the shadows. Vonn stops when he reaches the stairs that lead up to the stage. "Ready?" he calls.

I nod and then realize he probably can't see me. Just as I call out "I'm ready," Vonn flips a switch, and the ballroom comes to life! Suddenly, there is light blazing from glowing wall sconces and a massive chandelier. Covered in glittering crystals, it hangs from a ceiling painted with beautiful frescoes. I look up and see chubby brown angels floating on puffy white clouds. Then I look again and realize they aren't paintings! The cherubs are laughing and stuffing themselves with every kind of delicious food—tacos, cannoli, egg rolls, cheese fries, and red velvet cake.

Vonn taps my shoulder, and I finally pull my gaze

away from the ceiling. He leads me across the crowded floor of the ballroom. Folding chairs have been set up in rows with one main aisle down the middle. The trial obviously hasn't started yet because people are mingling and chatting over cups of coffee.

A trio of musicians plays mellow jazz softly onstage. Or maybe the music just sounds soft because the ballroom is buzzing with anticipation. Clearly, I'm not the only one who's nervous and excited about the trial. I don't see any other kids here, but there are all kinds of different adults. There are some people who look older than Ma, and plenty who look closer to Quayesha's age. Some look quite plain, and others have elaborate hairstyles, lots of makeup, and flashy jewelry. At least two people move about the room in chairs that hover above the floor instead of rolling on wheels. It looks like anyone and everyone can be a witch!

Folks seem to have come from every part of the world. Each person is wearing a unique outfit, but whatever they have on is color coded. As people mix and mingle, I start to feel like I'm looking through a kaleidoscope!

"Each coven has its own colors," Vonn explains.

Before I can ask him about Brooklyn's colors, I see a familiar face—it's Quayesha! I wonder if her beautiful dress is real or just an illusion caused by the glamour. Made from African fabric, her bright orange shift has large purple fish swimming through golden waves. Her long black locks are piled high atop her head and cascade down the side of her face.

I weave my way through the crowd to stand next to Quayesha. She pretends not to notice me at first and then acts surprised to see me.

"Jax! I didn't expect to see you here. Glad you could make it," Quayesha says with a sly wink.

"Thanks for helping me," I tell her. "I hope you won't get into trouble with Ma."

"Don't you worry 'bout me, Jax. I'll be all right. Look—there's Dutch," Quayesha says, nodding at a corner of the room.

Once I see Dutch, it's easy to figure out the Brooklyn coven's colors. Under her black pinstripe suit, Dutch wears a purple shirt with a bright orange tie. A matching silk handkerchief pokes out of her jacket pocket. I wave, and Dutch nods back as she lifts her pinstripe fedora. Judging by her smile, I think she's happy to see me, too.

I look down at my own blue jeans and black hoodie and wish I'd worn something else. Then I remember what Mrs. Benjamin said about me not belonging in their coven. I guess it doesn't matter what colors I wear.

"What you doing here, boy? Thought I told you to stay home."

Ma's voice sounds stern but not as angry as I feared. I take a deep breath and turn around to face her. She's with Mrs. Benjamin, and both older witches seem annoyed by the excitement in the room.

"Vonn brought me," I say.

"That so?" Ma asks, still facing me but shifting her dark eyes to Vonn.

He nods confidently and loops his arm around my neck in a protective, brotherly way. "Jax wanted to come—and he *was* summoned by the Supreme Council."

Mrs. Benjamin sucks her teeth but says nothing. She's wearing a dark purple wool skirt and an orange turtleneck. Ma is sporting a black velour tracksuit, but her voluminous white Afro is pushed back by a bright orange scarf dotted with purple flowers. Like Ma, Mrs. Benjamin has on sensible black shoes. Everyone else here might be going to a party, but these two look like they're ready to get to work.

"Do you know what a proxy is, Jax?"

I shake my head, and Ma offers me an explanation.

"It's someone who speaks or acts on your behalf. I'm here as the proxy for Sis. And I hoped you'd let me do the same for you."

"I can speak for myself," I say with more confidence than I knew I had.

Ma just grunts and turns away to speak to a short, round man with an important-looking badge on his suit jacket.

I didn't realize Dutch had joined us, but she puts her hand on my shoulder and says, "You got guts, Jax. I don't know too many people in this room who would stand up to Ma like that."

I feel a bit shaky inside, but I'm more nervous than afraid. "I'm not her apprentice anymore," I say to myself as much as anyone else. "Ma can't tell me what to do."

"No, she can't," Quayesha agrees. "But just because you're not part of our coven doesn't mean Ma no longer cares about you. Try to remember that, Jax."

Someone rings a bell, and the room grows quiet. The musicians take away their instruments, and three heavy wooden chairs are brought onstage. With their elaborate carving, they look a bit like thrones, but the three people who cross the stage to stand before them look surprisingly ordinary. Unlike everyone else in attendance, the three members of the Supreme Council wear plain black robes and simple silver hats.

They wait a moment for everyone in the ballroom to find a seat. I follow Dutch and Quayesha over to a row of chairs near the stage. There are seats left in our row, but Ma and Mrs. Benjamin choose to sit on the other side of the aisle. Dutch discreetly points at the council member on the left and says, "That's Judge Osaka. Her grandmother was a powerful shaman in Japan."

Quayesha fills me in on the other two councillors. "In the middle is Judge Wa Ehi Hoci—he's a respected elder and skillful Ho-Chunk healer—and last but not least is Judge Akpo. They say she's descended from the last king of Dahomey."

All three sound like important people, and yet their faces look kind. Maybe I'm just hoping that's how they'll be when it's my turn to stand before them. I expect to hear a gavel banged as the three judges call for order, but the room is already silent. The three Supreme Councillors have our undivided attention. I quickly check my phone to ensure that it's silenced. The phoenix stirs in my pocket, so I pull it out and let it sit on my shoulder for a while.

There are no microphones and the speakers don't

raise their voices, but everyone in the room can hear them.

Judge Wa Ehi Hoci begins. "As practitioners of magic, we acknowledge that we stand on the traditional unceded homelands of my people, the Ho-Chunk, as well as the Ojibwe, Odawa, Bodewadmi, Miami, Menominee, Sac, and Fox."

Judge Osaka speaks next. "We humbly thank our hosts for permitting us to hold these proceedings on their ancestral territory."

Judge Akpo smiles and concludes, "We recognize that their magic is ancient, forming a protective circle around all those gathered here today."

Dutch nudges me with her elbow, and I turn to see representatives from each American Indian tribe standing near the stage. They nod at the councillors, who bow solemnly in return and then take their seats.

"We are ready to proceed," Judge Osaka says. "Where is the complainant?"

Blue stands up and faces the three judges. "I'm here and ready to present my case, Your Honors."

"Take the stand," Judge Wa Ehi Hoci says with a wave of his hand.

Blue walks up the center aisle and steps onto a wooden box that has been placed before the stage. He doesn't look as laid-back as he did yesterday in the park, but Blue is clearly determined. He wears a black leather jacket over a white shirt and black jeans. I remember how he cowered in the corner the night his friends were taken, but Blue stands tall and proud now that Sis is far away in Palmara.

He clears his throat and begins. "The balance between the two realms has been upset. Sis, the self-appointed Guardian of Palmara, has blocked the flow of people, creatures, and ideas that has for millennia allowed this world and the world of magic to coexist peacefully. I'm sure many of you have noticed that the climate has taken a turn. Many elders across the country have succumbed to a worrisome sleeping spell. And the children who witnessed Sis's theft have developed certain . . . complications. So it is not only for myself that I raise this grievance. The future of magic is at stake."

Blue pauses, and a murmur ripples through the audience. It's hard to tell whether people agree with Blue or are shocked by his accusations. I wait to see if he will take responsibility for the sleeping spell and our new mutant abilities.

"Sis cannot be allowed to disregard the laws that our union has agreed to follow and that you, the Supreme Council, have vowed to uphold," Blue argues.

The councillors whisper among themselves before Judge Akpo says, "These are serious charges. The Guardian of Palmara is revered by our kind, but no one is above the law. Is Sis here to refute the claims against her?"

Ma grabs everyone's attention by pounding the hardwood floor with the tip of her cane. The three judges recognize her with a nod of their heads and Ma makes her way to the front of the stage. Dutch meets her there and helps Ma climb onto a second box. I quiver, knowing it should be me helping Ma right now. But I am not here as her apprentice—I am here to testify.

Blue faced the Supreme Council as he spoke, but Ma turns so that she can address everyone. "I have been asked to speak on behalf of the Guardian of Palmara. The charges made by this charlatan are false and designed solely to increase his own personal power. The sedation spell affecting the human population is not a result of Sis's actions—Blue himself cast the spell in order to create a climate of chaos and fear."

A second wave of sound washes over the assembly. It's still hard to tell whether the union members are impressed or shocked, but Blue just smiles and shakes his head dismissively.

Ma points an angry finger at him and yells, "The

delicate balance between realms has indeed been upset, but not by Sis. The creatures in her care were duped by Blue and trapped upon his body in the form of tattoos. Sis liberated them and restored them to their home in Palmara. Had she not acted decisively, this snake oil salesman would have continued to exploit the creatures by extracting their magical properties for profit."

The room crackles with energy, and this time I can tell that the crowd is turning against Blue. Those seated nearest his box push their chairs back so that it's clear he stands alone against Ma. Blue is no longer grinning, but he doesn't seem worried. He even looks over his shoulder to wink at me. My cheeks burn, and the witches seated around me shift their chairs as well as if to avoid contamination. Even with Vonn and Quayesha on either side of me, I feel vulnerable and alone. Maybe it was a mistake to come today. Maybe Ma was right to order me to stay at home.

Blue lifts his head defiantly and says, "*I* am not on trial here. *I* am here to demand justice for the creatures who were in my care. I consider them my friends, and they were cruelly wrenched from me without their consent. The Guardian must be held accountable for the laws she has broken."

"Sis did what was necessary to fulfill her sacred duty," Ma insists.

"How would you even know, old woman?" Blue snaps. "You weren't present that night. If I recall correctly, *you* had succumbed to the very spell for which you now blame me—a condition you brought upon yourself by removing three infant dragons from their birthplace."

"Is this true?" Judge Osaka asks.

Ma frowns. "It is true, Your Honor, that I was not present at the emporium on the night in question but—"

Judge Wa Ehi Hoci rudely interrupts Ma. "Then what evidence do you have to support your claims against this man?"

Before Ma can answer, Blue spins and points at me. "I have a corroborating witness! I ask that the council call Jaxon to the stand."

My stomach flips as all eyes in the room zero in on me. But somehow I manage to stand and walk up to a third box placed between Blue and Ma.

Without even looking at me, Ma begins to speak on my behalf. "This is—was—my apprentice. I ask that he be excused on account of his age and status as an uninitiated member of the community. He's just a boy. . . ."

I stand up taller and clear my throat. "I was there that night, Your Honors!"

Ma turns to me and shakes her head sadly. "You don't have to do this, Jax."

"I want to testify," I tell Ma. Then I turn to address the Supreme Council. "It's true that I don't know as much about magic as the rest of you, but this is *my* world, too. It's *my* friends who have been affected—and they're changing because they went to the emporium that night. But they only went there because *I* lost one of the baby dragons. I wanted to make things right, and they offered to help me. So I'm here to speak for them as well."

The councillors look at one another and seem satisfied with my first statement. Judge Akpo nods at me and, in a kind voice, says, "Proceed, young man."

I take a deep breath and think of what to say. "I'm only nine years old. I don't know what it was like when the two realms were linked—when people and creatures could go back and forth. When I first met Ma last spring, she told me that magic was leaving Brooklyn, and that made me sad. But when the dragons were born, I offered to help Ma take them back where they belong. The thing is, as soon as we tried to do that, everything started to go wrong. I took two of the dragons back to Palmara, but my friend's little sister stole the third one. She named it and fed it, and Mo started to grow. The transporters stopped working. . . . Ma fell into a deep sleep. . . . I didn't know what to do. And then I met Blue."

I turn and look at him, wondering once again if it's a mistake to trust this man. I can't bring myself to look at Ma right now, but I feel her eyes on me just the same. Part of me still wants to ask her for help. But I've started telling my story, the Supreme Council is listening, and I have to keep going until I reach the end.

"Everyone told me not to trust Blue—and that seemed like good advice at first. He's definitely . . . different from the other practitioners I know. Ever since I met Blue, he's had just one goal: to keep magic in our world. I know I'm just a kid, but from where I stand, that sounds like a really good idea.

"When you keep people apart just because they're different, that's not fair—and it stops us all from getting to know each other better. And if we don't get to know one another, we might start to feel afraid of the things that make us different.

"I know that Sis is the Guardian of Palmara. She's got a job to do. And there are a lot of things wrong with the world we live in. So many animals have gone extinct or are endangered. I don't blame Sis for wanting all the magical creatures to live someplace better. But it's true—they didn't want to be sent back to Palmara."

Blue nods approvingly at me and then sneers at Ma, so I hurry on. "But I also believe we could make this world better—safer—kinder to folks who are different than us. I mean, shouldn't we at least give it a try?"

I hear murmuring behind me, and it gives me the confidence to keep going. "The thing is, meeting people like Ma and Blue has changed me—for the better. I've learned stuff from my granddad Trub, too, and I know I could learn a lot more if there was someone willing to teach me. Being close to dragons and fairies and this baby phoenix"—I pause to point at the tiny bird on my shoulder—"has changed me and my friends, too. We're not just regular kids anymore. Kavita has started to look a bit like Mo, and she can even breathe fire! Kenny has started to levitate. He doesn't have wings yet, but he thinks he can figure out how to fly. And both of them—they can communicate with their friends in Palmara. So even though Sis has sealed all the gates, we're still connected to that realm."

"And what about you, young man? Have you been changed by your exposure to the residents of Palmara?"

I look at Judge Osaka and feel a knot in my belly. Blue said all I had to do was tell the truth—the whole truth, and nothing but the truth.

"Yes, Your Honor. I've been changed, too. This

phoenix was born only yesterday, but already I've absorbed some of its power. I don't know how or why—and to be honest, I could really use some advice because all of this is new to me. But if Sis were here, I know she'd want to take the phoenix away, when what I really need is someone to show me how to keep it safe.

"I don't think Sis is a bad person, and I don't know enough about your laws to say whether she's guilty or not. That's for you to decide. All I know is, this world belongs to all of us. The future is something we share, and everyone should have a say. One powerful person shouldn't be allowed to build a wall that divides us. If we want to get along, then what we really need is a bridge."

At first, I'm not sure what I'm hearing. A faint tapping sound starts slowly at the back of the room. Then it gets faster and louder, and by the time I turn around, almost everyone in the room is clapping. The sound is applause—and they're clapping for me!

13

When the applause dies down, the first thing I do is turn to look at Ma. She nods at me, and I nod back. There's something in her face that I haven't seen in a while. I think it's pride—or maybe it's respect. Even though we disagree about the future of magic, I think Ma's impressed with the way I delivered my statement. I'm proud of myself, too!

The three members of the Supreme Council quietly exchange remarks. I can't hear what they're saying, but they seem to have come to an agreement. Judge Wa Ehi Hoci holds up his hand, and the voices buzzing behind me grow quiet once more.

"For centuries we have trusted in the Guardian of Palmara. The charges made against her are serious and demand a response. We will summon Sis to appear before the Supreme Council immediately."

"That's impossible. Sis cannot come." Ma says this defiantly, without attempting to apologize.

Blue scoffs at Ma. "She *will not* come, you mean." He turns to address the councillors. His tone is respectful, but his words are barbed. "This is not the first time Sis has flouted the conventions of our union. She clearly believes that she alone is above the law."

"Sis is busy cleaning up the mess *you* created!" Ma fumes. "Many of the creatures you stole are unwell and must be nursed back to health."

Blue ignores her and appeals directly to the Supreme Council. "Might I propose an alternative? Only one person can speak to what truly motivates Sis, and that is not her dear friend Ma. I wish to call a second witness, as is my right. I wish to summon the person who knows the Guardian best—her twin brother, Ranadahy. Better known to many of you as Ol-Korrok."

The crowd erupts in cries of shock, outrage, and dismay. Chairs scrape and topple as some witches jump to their feet to object. The councillors try to calm the agitated audience, but their appeals can barely be heard above the din. I look over at Blue and see a sly grin spreading across his face.

Suddenly, a loud cawing adds to the chaos. People

scan every corner of the room, searching for the bird. Then someone cries, "There it is!" and all eyes swing up to the chandelier. The dangling crystals tinkle as a large crow perches on the lower tier of the giant lamp. At least, I think it's a crow. Its head and body are black, but the feathers on its breast and neck are white. The bird caws a few more times, and then the lights on the chandelier blink before going out completely. The wall sconces flicker as well but remain lit. The crowd murmurs anxiously.

Ma reaches for me. It's reassuring to have her hand on my shoulder because seconds later, a rush of air pours down on us like rain. The phoenix huddles close, and I use my hand to shield it from the gust of wind. The downward force of air clears a space in the center of the ballroom, and as the chandelier lights up once more, the crow lands on the floor. It is the crow, but it isn't. The moment its claws touch the floor, the bird spins and lengthens. In a flurry of black and white feathers, it morphs into a very tall man as I watch in awe. His skin is almost as dark as the crow's black feathers, and his bald head gleams. The man turns slowly, looking regal in a floor-length robe made of black silk. White feathers sprout from his collar, and under his robe he wears a long white tunic covered in elaborate silver embroidery.

Blue clears his throat and announces, "May I present Ol-Korrok, brother of Sis and the *rightful* ruler of Palmara."

Now facing the Supreme Council, the crow-man sweeps one arm back and bows so deeply that his bald head comes close to the ballroom floor. As he raises himself, his dark eyes fix on mine, and I shudder, recalling Kenny's message from Jef: *Beware the crow!*

Ol-Korrok strides up what's left of the aisle and effortlessly leaps onto the stage instead of standing before the councillors like me, Blue, and Ma. Somewhere behind me, I hear Mrs. Benjamin suck her teeth, and I don't blame her. It does seem rather presumptuous to share the stage with the Supreme Council—especially when his unusual height allows him to loom over the seated judges.

"Were you not banished from Palmara a thousand years ago?" Judge Akpo inquires.

Ol-Korrok nods and dramatically presses his palm to his chest as if to soothe his aching heart. "I have been alone for so very long. It is a pleasure to be here with you all on this solemn occasion."

For someone who's been locked in a tower, the wizard has surprisingly polished manners, and he's clearly at ease onstage. He moves and talks like an actor, waving his arms and twirling his cape for effect. I can tell Ma's not impressed, but everyone else seems mesmerized— including me.

"No doubt you have heard many unfavorable things

about me. It is true that I was forced into exile by my impetuous sister. For what crime, you ask? Nothing more than a sincere desire to serve Palmara and its precious residents. Once I was thrust out of her way, Ranabavy—or 'Sis,' as she came to be called—then proclaimed herself Guardian. It pains me to say it, but she has worked diligently ever since to destroy the ties that kept our realms close for thousands of years."

"Liar!"

Ma spits the word at the man onstage, and he responds as if struck by a poisoned arrow. His theatrics are a little over-the-top, but the audience is riveted by his performance.

Pressing the back of his hand to his brow, he laments, "So many hearts have been hardened against me! I realize that to some, my banishment must seem justified. To some, the truth is too much to bear." He pauses to stretch out his hand to Ma. "Believe me, madam, I understand your pain. Like you, I love my sister dearly, and it broke my heart when she seized Palmara for herself. I come before you now not to beg forgiveness, for I have committed no crime. I ask only that you consider this modest proposal."

Judge Osaka clears her throat and says, "I must ask,

sir, that you address the councillors directly and not the witnesses."

In a whirl of silk and feathers, Ol-Korrok spins to face the Supreme Council. "Of course, please forgive me. Sadly, I have spent too many years in isolation and have forgotten the conventions of polite society. My suggestion is this: since Sis will not subject herself to interrogation in this realm, why not send an emissary to Palmara?"

"An excellent idea!" Blue exclaims.

Ma frowns, but the councillors look intrigued.

"And what exactly would this emissary achieve?" Judge Wa Ehi Hoci asks.

"Well, the role of any ambassador is to represent abroad those who remain at home. What we need now is a sincere person of impeccable character who can negotiate with my sister—make her see that it is in the interest of both realms that the gates remain open. I have seen here today a model diplomat, someone who is earnest in his belief that our world, once unified, could prove hospitable to all living things. It is with complete confidence and no reservations whatsoever that I nominate . . . Jaxon."

Before I can even register the fact that Ol-Korrok is

pointing at *me,* Ma shouts, "Absolutely not! He's just a child."

"Ah, but Jax is no ordinary boy," Blue quickly counters. "The phoenix has endowed him with special abilities. Plus, he has already been to Palmara and is known to Sis."

Sis definitely knows who I am, but would she be happy to see me again? I doubt it—especially if my mission is to convince her to let her precious creatures return to our world.

"Would I have to go alone?" I ask.

"You're not going at all, and that's final," Ma barks at me.

"Madam, your resistance to this honest initiative puzzles me. Are you suggesting that my sister might harm the boy?" Mischief gleams in Ol-Korrok's eyes.

"I'm suggesting no such thing," Ma retorts. "If you're so keen to communicate with your dear sister, why don't *you* appeal to her yourself?"

The wizard hangs his head and is so overcome with emotion that he can barely speak. He rolls his lips in and holds up his finger, asking us for time so he can compose himself.

"Nothing would make me happier than to be reunited with my estranged sibling. I wish I could convey the devastation of having my beloved sister—my twin, my other half—so cruelly severed from my life. But if I were to appear in Palmara now, I fear Sis would be ruled by passion and not by reason. What we need is someone less threatening, who would go in a spirit of reconciliation, not confrontation."

Ma jerks her thumb at Blue. "Why not send him? He's clearly been your minion for some time now."

Blue looks down his nose at Ma and in a snooty voice says, "As Ol-Korrok just explained, the ambassador must be someone Sis will receive with open arms. I'm not likely to receive a warm welcome from the dragon lady." He then turns to address the councillors more respectfully. "I propose that Jax be sent to Palmara with his friends—they, too, have been blessed with extraordinary abilities. Together they would make a formidable team."

"This is not a game," Judge Akpo reminds Blue. "Can you offer any guarantees regarding the safety of these children?"

The question was asked of Ol-Korrok, but he sweeps his hand toward Blue as if to say, "After you." Blue isn't smiling, but there's something in the arrangement of his face that makes me feel like he's smirking inside.

"The youngsters can only be in jeopardy if Sis's

integrity is in question. If the esteemed members of the Supreme Council truly believe that the Guardian would endanger innocents in order to hold on to power, then I cannot in good conscience permit the mission to proceed."

"Sis wouldn't harm a hair on their heads, and you know it," Ma says angrily.

It's clear she understands the game Blue is playing. Ma doesn't want me to go to Palmara, but she also doesn't want to admit that Sis can be dangerous when she's mad. Finally, Ma sighs and says, "I will go instead of the boy."

Blue's mouth falls open, and for the first time, he doesn't have a ready response. He sputters for a moment but gathers his thoughts after Ol-Korrok glares at him.

"An ambassador must be impartial—your loyalty to Sis would cloud your judgment."

"What would *you* know about loyalty?" Ma snaps. "The boy is my apprentice. It is my duty to guide and protect him."

"Were you protecting him when you deliberately withheld the summons sent by the Supreme Council? If I hadn't run into Jax by chance yesterday, he wouldn't have known about the trial at all!" Blue exclaims dramatically.

Shocked by the accusation, the councillors frown at Ma. "Is this true?" Judge Osaka demands.

Ma looks at the floor, and I speak up to save her the embarrassment of admitting the truth. "I am no longer Ma's apprentice." I feel a quick stab of pain in my heart but manage to go on. "I've learned a lot from Ma, but it seems that becoming a witch isn't my destiny after all."

Judge Wa Ehi Hoci nods at me. "Do you willingly agree to undertake this mission on our behalf?"

I swallow hard and say, "I will accept this mission if my friends can accompany me. Blue's right—we do make a great team." I'm not sure if ambassadors have to take a vow, so I just add, "I promise that I will do all I can to convince Sis to reunite the realms."

Judge Akpo beams at me. "Then go with the blessing of the Supreme Council."

"We wish you every success, young man," adds Judge Osaka.

The three judges rise and leave the stage as the audience applauds.

"Young man," I hear Ma mutter to herself. "He's just a boy!" Then she flings a finger at Blue and hisses, "This is your fault, you weasel. If anything happens to those kids, you'll have ME to reckon with."

Still onstage, Ol-Korrok exclaims, "Marvelous!" With a thunderous clap of his hands, he concludes, "It's settled, then. Blue will see that our new ambassador has everything he needs, and I will go ahead and prepare the bridge."

"What bridge?" Ma asks warily. "Sis shut down the portals and closed all gates between the two realms."

Ol-Korrok just laughs. "She certainly tried, bless her." Then the smile slides off his face, and his dark eyes flash at Ma. "But where there's a will, there's always a way."

With that ominous warning, the wizard raises his fist above his head, snaps his fingers once, and spins himself into a black tornado. Within seconds, the black-and-white crow rises from the top of the swirling column. The bird squawks loudly in Blue's direction and then flies out of the ballroom, leaving a single black feather to slowly drift to the floor.

Familiar ringed fingers reach for it and offer it to me. I climb down from the witness box and accept the feather from Vonn. "Did you know Ol-Korrok would be here today?" I ask, glancing at Vonn's matching tattoo.

He nods and steps aside as Quayesha rushes up to

hug me. Dutch shakes my hand next, but when I turn to Ma, she just frowns and walks away with Mrs. Benjamin whispering in her ear.

I blink fast to clear the tears that rush to my eyes. "Guess I'm going to miss the gala tonight," I say with a wobbly smile.

"Just give her time," Dutch says, nodding in the direction Ma went. "She might not like it, but eventually Ma will accept the ruling of the Supreme Council. She has to."

Quayesha puts her pointy fingernail under my chin and lifts my head so she can look me in the eye. "You know what I love most about the world of magic?"

I shake my head, and Quayesha leans in closer. Her breath smells like grape bubble gum.

"There's room for everyone—and that includes you, Jax. Just 'cause you're not in our coven doesn't mean we won't look out for you."

"That's right, Junior," Dutch says, giving my shoulder a playful punch. "If you ever need a lift, the UR is at your disposal."

That gives me an idea. "Actually, I do need to pick up my friends back in Brooklyn. And I need to say goodbye to my mom."

"I'm ready when you are," Dutch says with a smile. "And with that feathery fireball in your pocket, we'll be back in Chicago before you know it."

"No more hiccups?" I ask with a sly grin.

"Now that the phoenix has hatched, its energy isn't trapped. This time the ride will definitely feel like a slingshot. Round trip in an hour—maybe less."

The phoenix chirps happily and gives my neck an affectionate rub. Suddenly, Blue bursts into our circle, rubbing his palms together and grinning from ear to ear.

"I see you've already started to plan your mission. You're better than a Boy Scout, Jax! I need to head downtown to open the gate, so I'll take my leave now. Vonn, please deliver Jax and his friends to Millennium Park by, shall we say, nine o'clock?"

Vonn nods and walks off with Blue to discuss our departure. Quayesha and Dutch escort me out of the ballroom. As soon as we head downstairs, the glamour starts to wear off, and the Forum returns to its dilapidated condition. Quayesha and Dutch magically switch back to the clothes they were wearing when they left the rooming house this morning.

"What about the gala?" I ask.

"I'm going home to change right now," Quayesha tells

me. "Dutch can change and meet me here when she gets back from Brooklyn."

I wait until we're out on the street before calling Vik and Kenny. I don't divulge too many details, but my friends trust me, and we agree to meet at the lamppost in Prospect Park. Once we're face to face, I'll explain everything. I've already committed myself to the mission, but I really hope Kenny and Vik will come along.

Before I hang up, I make one request. "Kenny— remember when Jef managed to connect us with L. Roy using that sphere?"

"Sure, I remember. Why?"

"Think you could do the same thing on your own?" I ask. "I really need to talk to L. Roy."

"I'll give it a try," Kenny promises, though he sounds less than confident. "What should I ask?"

"I need to reach my grandfather, so just see if L. Roy knows where he is."

"Got it. See you soon, Jax."

I hang up and consider calling Mama next, when I sense someone standing behind me. I turn and find Ma and Mrs. Benjamin waiting to speak to me. I'm not sure what to say, but Mrs. Benjamin surprises me by taking the lead. She reaches for my face and holds her rough palm against my cheek for a moment. Then she looks into my eyes and almost manages to smile at me.

"You're a brave boy, Jaxon. Not everyone could so easily embrace a new destiny."

"I didn't have much choice," I tell her.

Mrs. Benjamin twists her lips and grabs hold of my chin. "You *always* have a choice. Remember that, boy."

I nod, and she releases me. Ma steps forward, and Mrs. Benjamin goes over to join Dutch and Quayesha.

"I think you're making a mistake," Ma says with a sigh. "But I just want you to know that you can always come to me if you need help. I may not be your boss anymore, but I'll always be your friend, Jax."

I blink fast to stop the tears that are threatening to fall. I'm an ambassador now, with important responsibilities. I don't have time to cry on Ma's shoulder.

I clear my throat, but my question still comes out quieter than I hoped. "Did you ever believe that I could become a witch someday?"

Ma doesn't have eyebrows, but the wrinkles above her eyes go up. "Course I did! Soon as your mama handed you over to me that day, I knew you had potential. But there were signs that you were meant to do something else, and signs can't be ignored."

"What kind of signs?"

"Mrs. Benjamin has the gift of second sight. She knew long before she ever laid eyes on you that it wasn't meant to be. Even Sis told me back in Palmara that you weren't cut out for the job, but I thought we could prove her wrong. And you impressed us all by tracking down the stolen dragon. You brought me out of my sleeping spell. I thought we could make it work."

"Then why did you stop teaching me how to become a witch?"

Ma sighs heavily. I'm not sure I've ever seen her look so tired. "Mrs. Benjamin knew you'd never join our coven, but even after consulting her bones, she couldn't see exactly where you'd end up. If I gave you certain skills . . . if I taught you how to handle magic, there was no way to know how you might use it once you left me."

My stomach sinks. "But . . . I'd never do anything to hurt you, Ma."

"Not on purpose—no. But you're special, Jax, and I'm not the only one who's figured that out. People may try to get close to you, to influence you. . . ." Ma shrugs. "I know you wanted to learn spells, and I was sorry to disappoint you. I tried to teach you things that might help you no matter what path you found yourself on. Things that would help and not harm others."

"Yesterday I found some silver root growing in

Washington Park," I tell her. "My friend's grandmother needed something to stop her from falling asleep."

Ma nods, and I think I see a glimmer of pride in her weary eyes. "You got a good heart, Jax. You genuinely want to help others, so let that impulse guide you. When you find yourself wondering what to do, ask yourself what would help most."

I swallow hard and say, "I will, Ma. I promise."

Just as I open my arms to give Ma a farewell hug, a sleek black sedan with tinted windows and spinning rims pulls up to the curb. Vonn gets out of the driver's side and comes around to open the back door. Mrs. Benjamin gets in first, and then Ma slowly shuffles over to the car. Vonn tries to help her, but Ma irritably shrugs his hand off her elbow. She tosses her cane into the back seat and grabs hold of the roof and the open door to steady herself.

Suddenly, all the tears I've been blinking away and holding back start pouring out of my eyes. It's like a dam has burst inside of me, and with a silent sob, I throw myself at Ma's back. For a few seconds she lets me lock my arms around her puffy coat. I want to say something—*anything*—but I can't get any words out.

"Time to let go," Ma says quietly.

Quayesha gently peels my arms away so Ma can

finally get in the car. I'm blubbering like a baby just a few feet away, but Ma looks straight ahead. Vonn closes her door and opens the front one.

Quayesha hugs me tight and kisses the top of my head. "Everything's going to be all right, Jax. I promise."

Then she climbs into the front seat, and Vonn closes her door, too, before going back over to the driver's side.

"I'll see you later, Brooklyn," he calls before slipping into the car and driving away.

Dutch puts her arm around my shoulder and tells me it's time for us to leave, too.

"Come on, Junior. Your carriage awaits."

14

By the time we reach the elevator hidden inside the George Washington monument, the tears on my face have dried. Dutch doesn't try to chat or cheer me up. She just lets me be sad for a while.

Dutch was right about the ride back to Brooklyn. Just as I nod off and hear the strange man from my dreams—"The wait is almost over, my son"—the UR glides to a halt under Prospect Park.

Dutch swivels in her conductor's seat and nudges my foot with her own. "You awake, Junior?"

I yawn, stretch, and check my phone. It's quarter past seven. We left Chicago just before six and there's a one-hour time difference. "You weren't kidding—we got here in less than half an hour!" I exclaim. Then I turn to the dozing phoenix and say, "Thanks, little buddy." There are other benefits to being around such a powerful energy source—I haven't had to charge my phone once since the phoenix hatched!

"So—what's the plan?" Dutch asks.

My throat still feels a bit raw, so I pull the water bottle out of my knapsack and take a few sips. What *is* my plan? How will I convince Mama to let me go to Palmara on my own? Trub is already over there, but I have a feeling he might be in trouble, which means he can't help me if *I* end up in trouble, too.

"I should probably go home, but . . ."

Dutch seems to read my mind. "When it comes to magic," she says, "I keep most folks on a need-to-know basis. How much does your mom really need to know about your mission?"

I think for a moment. I guess Mama doesn't need to know that Ma won't be going with me. I could tell her that the Supreme Council declared it safe for me and my friends to travel to Palmara on our own. That should reassure Mama, shouldn't it?

"Of course, you could always send her a text instead," Dutch suggests. "Saying goodbye in person can be messy sometimes."

I blush a little, remembering the scene I made outside the Forum. "You're right. I'll text my mother before we head back to Chicago. Ma will be home in a day or two, and she can explain everything to Mama. That just leaves my friends. I asked them to meet me at the lamp-post next to the tunnel at seven-thirty."

Dutch stands and says, "You better not keep them waiting."

By tugging a tree root snaking out of the earthen wall of the cavern, Dutch brings down the paving stone staircase. I dash up it in search of my friends and find them standing in a pool of golden light at the mouth of the tunnel.

"Jax!"

I run into the open arms of Vik, Kenny, and Kavita. We're so happy that we're hugging and hopping and dancing in a circle. Finally, we relax and release one another.

"I missed you all—a lot," I say with a smile so wide it makes my face ache. "There's someone I want you to meet." I pull down my hood to reveal the tiny phoenix snuggling against my neck.

Kavi gasps. "It's so cute!"

"It's not much bigger than Jef," Kenny remarks.

"I see you've figured out how to keep your feet on the ground," I say.

Kenny laughs and says, "I'm finally getting the hang of it, I think. When you said you were going on another mission, I was hoping you'd ask us to come along. It's a good time to get outta Brooklyn."

"Because of the sleeping spell?" I ask.

Kenny nods. "New Yorkers can handle just about anything, but no one besides us knows what's causing so many grown-ups to fall asleep. The mayor's told everyone to stay inside, but not everyone's following his advice."

"Neighbors are looking out for each other, though," Vik says. "I saw one man who went to mail a letter, and he fell asleep on top of the mailbox! His address was on the letter, so some kind strangers took him home."

"I don't think it'll last much longer," I say hopefully. "Blue just wanted to make a point."

"What *is* the point?" Vik demands impatiently.

"He wants kids to have a say about the future of our world. This is our chance—we can go to Palmara and persuade Sis to unite the realms."

"Yes!" Kavi cries. "I want to see Aunty and Mo again. I miss them so much!"

"So do I, Kavi," Vik says calmly. "But how are we going to get there? I thought Sis sealed all the portals?"

"She did, but . . . her brother, Ol-Korrok, has found a way to move between the realms. It's some sort of bridge," I explain.

Kavi's eyes open wide. "Sis has a brother?"

I nod. "They're twins! But they had a big fight a long time ago, and Sis locked him up in a tower so she could rule Palmara on her own. He escaped somehow, though, because he was at the trial today." I open my mouth to tell them about Ol-Korrok's amazing transformation from a bird into a man. Then I think about the warning Jef passed on to Kenny and change my mind.

"Whoa," Kenny says. "That's some serious family drama."

Kavi still seems excited about the journey, but Vik looks skeptical. "What if we cross the bridge and can't get back again?" he asks. "What if it's a trap?"

I hurry to reassure him. "It can't be a trap. Ol-Korrok wants us to liberate the creatures Sis stole and bring them back to this world."

Vik frowns and folds his arms across his chest. "What about what *Sis* wants? Has anyone considered that? I don't suppose she'll just let us walk into Palmara and take the creatures she's meant to protect—especially if she finds out we're working for the brother she hates."

Everything Vik just said makes sense, but I still try to persuade him. "Technically, we'd be there on behalf of the Supreme Council. And we have special powers now. We can stand up to Sis."

Vik isn't convinced. "She can turn into a giant dragon, Jax. Remember?"

Kavi laughs. "Ha! So can I . . . sort of. I'm not scared of Sis," she says, planting her hands on her hips. "Someone has to help Mo and the others. I say we take a vote. All in favor of rescuing the magical creatures, raise your hand."

Kavi sticks her hand up and Kenny does, too. I want to raise my hand, but first I have to make sure my friends know why.

"There's something else—something I haven't told you."

"What?" Vik asks warily.

"I have to go to Palmara because I have to find Trub. I think he needs my help."

Vik unfolds his arms. "What happened?"

"I'm not sure," I admit before turning to Kenny. "Were you able to open a communication bubble?"

Kenny shakes his head. "Sorry, Jax. I think I need wings to do that. Remember when Jef did it? He beat his wings really fast."

"Probably to generate energy," Kavi says.

Suddenly, I remember what Dutch called the phoenix: a "feathery fireball."

"I've got an energy source," I tell my friends. I lift the

phoenix from my own shoulder and set it on Kenny's. "Try opening a bubble now," I urge him.

Kenny takes a deep breath and closes his eyes. We all step back to give him more room. Kenny stands on the tips of his toes and then lifts a few inches off the ground. He raises his arms above his head like a ballet dancer and then draws a circle in the air with his hands.

"It's working!" Kavi cries.

She's right—a large violet sphere has formed in front of Kenny. It floats like a bubble, and then we hear a man's voice.

"Who's there? Can you hear me?"

"L. Roy!" I cry. "It's Jax. I'm here in Brooklyn with my friends, but we're coming to Palmara. I need to speak to my grandfather. Is he with you?"

L. Roy looks a little shifty with his eyes darting back and forth behind his round spectacles. He tugs at his white mustache and says, "Uh . . . no . . . Trub isn't here right now. Can I take a message?"

Now I'm really starting to worry. "Is he okay?" I ask.

L. Roy clears his throat and says, "Sure! I mean, probably. I haven't heard from him in a while, but Trub can take care of himself."

I shake my head. "I think he needs our help, L. Roy."

"Well, er, that might be true. Sis sent him out on a

mission a few days ago, and . . . well, no one's heard from him since."

"I knew it!" I say to my friends. "Something's happened to Trub." I turn back to the bubble. "We'll be there soon, L. Roy. But don't tell Sis."

He just laughs. "Boy, I can't keep secrets from the Guardian. Besides, she already knows you're coming— and that you'll be crossing a bridge designed by her brother. I've been appointed head of the welcoming committee, so I'll see you soon."

The violet bubble dissolves as Kenny drifts back to earth and drops his weary arms. "Phew!" he cries. "That sphere sure was heavy."

I pat him on the back and say, "You did great, Kenny! Thanks for that." Then I turn to the others, but really, I'm talking to Vik.

"So, you see, I *have* to go. I'm not just an ambassador— I'm a grandson, too, and my grandfather needs me."

For a moment, none of us says anything. Then Kenny throws his arm around my shoulder.

"I don't trust Sis *or* her brother, but I'm definitely going with you!" he declares.

Kavi turns to Vik and clasps her hands together. "Please, Vik," she begs. "*Please* come with us. I know I haven't been myself lately . . . and I know I get you into trouble sometimes. But I really think I can help this time. And I know that Aunty will show me how to control my temper. If she can train a dragon like Mo, then she can train me, too," Kavi adds with a smile.

Vik looks from Kavi to Kenny to me. "I want to help, Jax, but I don't have magical powers like the rest of you. Are you sure you even need me on this mission?" he asks doubtfully.

"Yes!" I insist. "We need someone who thinks things through and doesn't lose their temper. I need someone loyal that I can trust. That's you, Vik."

Kavi takes her brother's hand and says, "I know I don't always listen to you, but you're the smartest boy I know, Vik."

Kenny throws his other arm around Vik and draws us closer together. "Don't quit the team, Vik! If there are four of us, maybe we could split up when we get to Palmara. I'll go with Kavi to talk to Sis, and you can help Jax find his grandfather," Kenny suggests.

Vik smiles and says, "Sounds like a plan, Kenny."

We do another group hug, and then it's time to head belowground.

"Ready to go?" I ask.

"Ready!" they reply.

I'm so grateful for my friends that I almost start crying again.

"I told my mom I was sleeping over at Vik's place," Kenny says with a sheepish grin.

Vik chuckles. "And we told our parents that we were staying over at Kenny's house. That means we've only got one day before they figure out that we lied and start to worry."

"I don't know how long this job will take," I tell them, "but Dutch has a theory about time. We can ask her to explain it on the way to Chicago."

As we leave the circle of light cast by the lamppost and head into the darkness of the tunnel, I turn to take one last look at my beloved Brooklyn. I'm not sure if we'll be back in a day or a week. I don't know if we'll be able to find my grandfather or convince Sis to reunite the two realms. But I know that whenever I do get back to Brooklyn, I probably won't be the same kid I am now.

"Look—a staircase!" Kavi cries from within the tunnel.

I hurry to catch up with my friends, and together we slip underground to embark on a new adventure in the realm of magic.

15

Before following my friends down the spiral staircase, I send Mama a quick text.

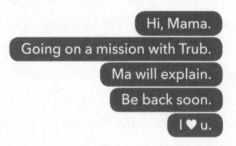

> Hi, Mama.
> Going on a mission with Trub.
> Ma will explain.
> Be back soon.
> I ♥ u.

It's not entirely true, but I figure it's all Mama needs to know right now.

Dutch is waiting for us at the bottom of the stairs. "Ready to go?" she asks before pulling the tree root that seals us underground.

I nod and introduce my friends to our conductor.

Then I lead them over to the UR and show them how to board.

"This is so cool," Kavi says as she steps through the UR's soft, clear shell.

"Are we allowed to eat in here?" Kenny asks once we're seated around the table.

"Buckle up first," Dutch says. She puts the UR in reverse and then swivels her seat so that she's facing us. Within seconds, the UR is rocketing back along the same route it took from Chicago.

It's been a while since I've had a proper meal, so I'm happy when Kenny opens his knapsack and pulls out some sandwiches. Vik takes a couple of juice boxes out of his bag and sets them on the table. The only thing I have to share is gum. I open a packet and hand a green gumball to Kavi after she begs to feed the phoenix.

"What's its name?" she asks as the tiny bird flutters from my shoulder to the table. It cautiously sniffs Kavi's palm before digging its beak into the green orb.

"I don't know," I reply. As Kenny puts more food on the table, I tell my friends about Itzel and how the phoenix seemed to understand K'iche'. "Everyone says this bird is ancient, even though it was just born a couple of days ago. Maybe in a few more days I'll be able to communicate with it the way you can with Jef."

Kenny nods and says, "It's possible." Then he sets his bag aside and asks, "Who's hungry? I figured we might need fuel for our mission, so I packed a few things."

I reach for half of a sloppily made sandwich, too hungry to care about how it looks. Vik takes the other half, and Kavi opens a bag of chocolate chip cookies. Kenny just watches us eat for a moment before offering a warning.

"I hope that sandwich tastes okay. You know my mom's always trying to get me to eat healthy stuff." He picks up half of the second sandwich and offers the rest to Dutch, who eyes it suspiciously before declining. Kenny takes a gigantic bite and while his mouth is still full says, "This may look like chicken salad, but it's not. And those cookies are sugar-free."

I swallow my first bite. "Tastes like chicken to me," I tell him.

Vik seems to agree, and despite her craving for sweets, Kavi looks satisfied with her snack. I know we'll be in Chicago before long, so I decide to ask Dutch a question.

"Hey, Dutch. Mrs. B. said you have a weird theory about time."

Dutch laughs and tilts her chair back. A footrest pops up, and she reclines before answering my question. "I can't really take credit for it," she says. "I heard this griot give a talk a while back, and I've thought about her ideas ever since. Have you ever seen the sankofa bird? It's an adinkra symbol from the Akan."

None of us knows about the bird, so Dutch describes it. "It's moving forward but looking back over its shoulder. What if we humans did that, too—moved forward while keeping an eye on the past? It's possible if you give up the idea of monochronic time. That's where one event happens after another."

"But . . . isn't that how time actually works?" Kenny asks while munching on a cookie.

I have a different question. "What's the alternative?"

Dutch gets excited and tilts her chair up again. She leans forward and rests her elbows on her knees. "Some cultures are polychronic—they believe multiple things can happen at the same time. So you don't have to wait for one thing to end before another begins."

Kavi frowns and loudly sucks the last bit of juice out of her box. "Everything happens all at once? That sounds messy."

Dutch laughs. "Some people like everything to happen according to a schedule. But some of us . . ." She shrugs and winks at me. "Some of us like to color outside the lines. All right, y'all. You better finish up your little feast—we're almost there."

We tidy up the table and store the leftovers in our bags. The phoenix looks sleepy, so I tuck it inside my pocket.

Dutch brings the UR to a smooth stop and looks at her phone. "Vonn texted to say he'll meet you all upstairs at eight."

"We better not keep him waiting," I tell my friends before turning to Dutch. "Thanks for the ride."

"Maybe I better go upstairs with you," Dutch says, reaching to undo her seat belt.

"That's okay," I assure her. "We'll be fine on our own."

"You sure?"

Kavi nods and shakes hands with Dutch before exiting the UR. Vik and Kenny follow her out but turn to wait for me at the bottom of a steep flight of stone steps.

"I'm sure, Dutch. I really appreciate you taking me all the way to Brooklyn and back. Plus, it's getting late— I don't want you to miss the gala."

Dutch grins and holds out her hand for me to shake, too. "Okay, Junior. Good luck in Palmara. We'll be rooting for you."

I wonder who Dutch means by "we," but I don't stop

to think about whether or not Ma wants me to succeed. Instead, I push through the wall of the UR and join my friends.

"Looks like the only way is up," Kenny says, sweeping his flashlight over the stairs. He takes a deep breath and starts to float up the staircase.

Kavi tries to beat Kenny and reaches the top just a moment before he does. Vik and I are halfway up the stairs when we hear Kavi breathlessly announce, "The door's stuck!"

Kenny lands and tries to help Kavi. When we get to the top of the staircase, Vik and I also grab hold of the large metal ring attached to the stone door. All four of us pull as hard as we can, and slowly the door begins to budge.

"I guess this stop hasn't been used in a while," I tell my friends. Dutch did say that Millennium Park was built not that long ago and that's why it didn't have an UR stop. She dropped us at the Art Institute instead, which is supposed to be close by.

It takes a lot of effort to move the heavy stone slab, but when it finally opens, violet light seeps into the tunnel. I squeeze through the narrow opening and look up at the starry purple sky. "I think we're between realms," I tell my friends.

Aside from the sky, everything looks normal. The stone door has opened into a small park next to the art museum. I look around for Vonn, but he's nowhere to be found. To my left is a stone boy holding a big blue fish. I suspect water would normally be flowing from the fish's open mouth, but the shallow fountain is empty. Above me I hear hushed voices and look up to find five bluish-brown women whispering and pointing at me.

"It's a boy!" one cries with delight.

I wave and say, "Uh . . . hello. I'm Jax. Have you seen my friend Vonn?"

The women set down the giant clamshells they were holding and pull their long, loose robes around them so they can climb down to my level. I reach out my hand to help one of the women. She thanks me and says, "You're the first to visit us in a very long time."

"Is it okay to come out?" Vik asks, poking his head around the stone door.

Before I can answer, Kavi pushes past her brother and jumps down into the dry fountain. Her mouth falls open when she sees the blue women. "Are you goddesses?" Kavi asks, awestruck.

The women giggle. One gently cups Kavi's face and says, "No, dear. We're water nymphs. I'm Michigan, and these are my sisters, Huron, Erie, Ontario, and Superior."

"The Great Lakes!" Vik cries.

His voice echoes through the empty park. I scan the lanes and benches once more, worried Vonn's camouflage outfit might make him hard to spot.

"I guess your friend stood us up," Kenny says.

I frown and turn to the nymphs. "Maybe you could help us. We're trying to get to Millennium Park, and we don't have much time."

"It isn't far," the tallest woman tells me. She takes my

hand in hers, and three other nymphs offer their hands to Kenny, Kavi, and Vik. The fifth woman walks ahead. We hear her whistle loudly, and by the time we reach the street, two giant green lions are waiting for us.

"Don't be afraid," the tall nymph says with a smile as the big cats swagger toward us. She affectionately strokes the manes of both creatures before giving them instructions. "Take these children directly to Cloud Gate." They nod at her, and we wave goodbye to the nymphs before heading up Michigan Avenue with our impressive feline escorts.

"We're a pride now," Kavi says with a grin. Kenny laughs and lifts off the ground every few steps to practice his flying skills.

"Wasn't your friend supposed to meet us?" Vik asks anxiously.

"Something must have come up," I tell him, trying not to look as worried as I feel.

We pass the Art Institute and see the empty plinths where the bronze lions usually stand guard. The streets are eerily empty, and I almost wish the kind nymphs were still there to hold our hands. What if I made a mistake trusting Blue? What if Vik was right and I've led my friends into some sort of trap?

We cross the street and pass a strange installation in

the park on our right. Two towers made of glass blocks face each other at the end of a paved space about the size of a basketball court. Both have long rectangular screens that crackle with static. Suddenly, the glass blocks are filled with golden light, and we hear a familiar voice. The static vanishes, and I jump in surprise as Blue's giant face appears on one tower and Vonn's on the other. Though they're facing each other, it's clear that they're both speaking to me.

"Sorry I couldn't make it, Brooklyn. Something came up."

"That happens a lot with you," I say without bothering to conceal my wariness.

"It's my fault," Blue admits. "I needed Vonn's assistance with another matter. But have no fear, kids," he says with a smile. "All the necessary preparations have been made. The gate is open—all you have to do is cross over to the other side."

"Into Palmara?" I ask.

"Not quite," Blue replies. "You'll reach Palmara eventually, but first you have to cross the bridge."

My friends look from Blue's face to mine. I know they're waiting for me to make the next move. Even the lions are looking at me expectantly. Blue's gray eyes taunt me—it's like he knows how much I want to be a leader but inside I'm struggling with doubts. I glance at Vonn, but as always, his dark shades conceal his eyes.

Finally, I take a deep breath to steady my voice and say, "We're ready." Then I turn to check with my friends. "Right?"

They nod, and we follow the lions farther up the block. I glance over my shoulder in time to catch one last message from Vonn. "You've always had the power to help others, Jax. Don't ever forget that."

Then both screens go blank, and we're on our own once more. The lions turn off Michigan Avenue and lead us up a path surrounded by flower beds. There are three moons in the sky—one full, one half, and one crescent—and the fragrant blossoms seem to dance in the light cast from above. In the real world, before Blue cast the sleeping spell, this park was a major tourist destination. All these empty lanes and terraces would have been packed with people wanting to see Cloud Gate. But tonight, in this space between realms, we have the silver bean all to ourselves.

It's a lot bigger than I imagined. In the postcard my dad sent me, tourists mill around the beautiful sculpture, stopping underneath it to gaze up at their own reflection. And that's exactly what we're doing now.

"So cool . . . ," Kavi says as she spreads her fingers and reaches out to grasp her own hands.

Kenny lifts off the ground and actually manages to touch the bean's mirrored surface. "It's cold," he tells us before coming back down.

Suddenly, the wind picks up, and we all shiver. It gets so chilly that we huddle together to keep warm.

"What's happening?" Vik whispers in my ear.

"The gate must be opening," I tell him, even though I'm not really sure what's going on. Then I hear a voice that raises the hair on the back of my neck.

"You're here at last."

We look around, but the plaza is empty.

"I've been waiting for you, my son."

My heart starts to race—it's the man from my dreams! I look up at the silver bean and see Ol-Korrok looking back at me.

"It's you!" I cry.

His dark eyes fix on mine, and his wide smile warps into a sneer. Then Ol-Korrok opens his mouth and starts to laugh. He spreads his arms wide as if to gather us in an embrace, but then his laughter becomes maniacal, and black feathers start to drip from his arms like tar.

Kavi buries her face in Vik's arm. Kenny gasps and breathes out Jef's warning: *Beware the crow.* . . .

"It *is* a trap!" Vik moans.

"N-no. It—it can't be," I stammer, but it looks like my friends were right not to trust Blue. They're here because they chose to trust *me,* and now I've put them in danger.

The wind howls around us, and we cringe as the massive bean starts to turn itself inside out. The arc above us comes closer and closer, pressing against us until we're lying flat on the ground. Then Ol-Korrok's laughter stops, and there is only darkness as the mirror sucks us inside. The last thing I hear is my friends' frantic cries and the wizard's voice saying, "You . . . are . . . welcome."

My last thought before I am swallowed is of Ma. She would know what to do, but Ma can't help me now. There is no one to save me and I can't help my friends because I am no longer the witch's apprentice.

ACKNOWLEDGMENTS

I am often asked by young readers which of the books I have written is my favorite. That particular "f-word" always makes me cringe; I have a favorite color (purple), but I can't really say that I love one thing more than any other, and I definitely don't do that with my own books. I generally tell kids that each book is distinct in my memory—I've written close to a hundred stories at this point, and for most, I can remember who and where I was at the moment of creation.

The Witch's Apprentice will always stand out as my pandemic novel. I moved from central Pennsylvania to Evanston, Illinois, in August 2020; I had never been to Evanston, and I signed a lease on an apartment that I had only viewed on YouTube. Fortunately, my new home turned out to be perfect for me, and my proximity to Chicago made it easy to do research for this novel, the third in my dragon series.

As a newcomer, I enjoyed exploring the city, but I also relied heavily on the expertise of my local friends. Natalie Bennett recommended Evanston as a potential home; she generously shared her knowledge of the South Side, connected me with Essence McDowell and Lakeesha Harris, and helped me find a place for Jaxon to have his first taste of deep-dish pizza. I ordered a copy of Essence's guidebook *Lifting as They Climbed: Mapping a History of Black Women on Chicago's South Side* (coauthored with Mariame Kaba); when its delivery was delayed, Monica Horton sent me photos of the map in her copy of the guidebook so I could proceed with my research and easily locate Elam House (the inspiration for Miss Ellabelle's Home for Working Women and Girls). After my copyeditors flagged the use of *Chi-Town* in the novel as possibly outdated among locals, I went to Monica again; she and Ebony Wilkins polled their friends and assured me that *Chi-Town* was still in use.

Satia Orange forwarded online events about Chicago history and treated me as though we'd been neighbors forever, even driving to Evanston for a quick curbside chat. Elisa Gall also welcomed me to Evanston and told me about the children's memorial to Breonna Taylor along the Midway; Madeline was one of Elisa's kindergarten students at the University of Chicago Laboratory

School, and her artwork inspired the fictional tribute Jax sees while touring the city with Vonn.

After taking the Chicago Architecture Center's boat tour on my birthday with Cozbi A. Cabrera and her daughter Jana, I became a member and, through the CAC's Open House Chicago, discovered the Forum in Bronzeville. It's an imposing building with an impressive history. Urban Juncture Foundation is raising funds to repair the roof; you can donate and/or learn more about this historic building at theforumbronzeville.com. Having Cozbi for a neighbor again has been such a blessing, and I'm thankful for our weekly walks, where I have space to reflect on (and rant about) the creative process and the publishing industry.

Though the pandemic kept us apart, I received support from many friends in distant places. My historian friend Christian Crouch urged me to include Black women's contribution to the 1893 World's Fair. Lakeesha Harris shared her perspective as a Black witch and reminded me that one cannot heal oneself without also serving one's community. I appreciated Gilles Perrine's introduction to Miora Razafiarivony, who verified my use of Malagasy terms for brother and sister (Ranadahy and Ranabavy). I met Gilles through his mentor, David Thompson, who is the husband of my longtime friend and unofficial editor Kate Foster. Kate read the manuscript, and her feedback helped clarify my vision for the series.

Maya Gonzalez and Matthew Smith once again generously shared their expertise when I had questions about nonbinary representation. Josee Starr (Arikara, Omaha, Odawa), education coordinator at the Mitchell Museum of the American Indian, introduced me to Ben Krause-Decorah (Ho-Chunk). Ben's review of the manuscript helped me to respectfully represent local Native American history and culture. Ben also provided assistance with the K'iche' language; my friend Mwangi Wa Githini shared useful information about the Maasai word for *crow* (Ol-korrok); and Purvi Shah once again reviewed my use of Gujarati phrases in the book. I very much appreciate their support but take sole responsibility for any errors I may have made.

For a long while, I believed I would have to self-publish *The Witch's Apprentice*. My fearless agent, Johanna Castillo, was ready to fight on my behalf, but I kept hearing Nina Simone's voice in my head: "You've got to learn to leave the table when love's no longer being served." After the global protests of 2020, many corporations pledged their support for the Black Lives Matter movement, but after decades of unequal treatment, Black creatives were skeptical. I'm glad that Random House invited me back to the table, acted on their stated commitment to equity, and decided to continue my Dragons in a Bag series. It was great having another chance to partner with my editor, Diane Landolf, and I appreciate the increased support of the Random House team. Stories have kept many of us connected throughout the pandemic, and I hope my fantasy fiction helps readers of all ages think more deeply about the new world we can imagine and build together.